# SHERLOCK HOLMES

Jaico Sherlock Holmes Series

## *The* LAST CONFESSION

# SHERLOCK HOLMES

## *The* LAST CONFESSION

KIERAN LYNE

JAICO PUBLISHING HOUSE

Ahmedabad Bangalore Chennai
Delhi Hyderabad Kolkata Mumbai

Published by Jaico Publishing House
A-2 Jash Chambers, 7-A Sir Phirozshah Mehta Road
Fort, Mumbai - 400 001
jaicopub@jaicobooks.com
www.jaicobooks.com



Published in arrangement with
MX Publishing Ltd
335 Princess Park Manor
London, N11 3GX

To be sold only in India, Bangladesh, Bhutan,
Pakistan, Nepal, Sri Lanka and the Maldives.

SHERLOCK HOLMES
THE LAST CONFESSION
ISBN 978-81-8495-708-2

First Jaico Impression: 2015



Page design and layout: SÜRYA, New Delhi

Printed by
Repro India Limited, Mumbai

*To Ra'ad,*
*for being there every step of the way.*

# CONTENTS

# ACKNOWLEDGEMENTS

FIRST AND FOREMOST I must thank Sir Arthur Conan Doyle for providing us all with these timeless characters: I can only hope I have done them justice. 'The characters of Sir Arthur Conan Doyle are used here by the kind permission of Jonathan Clowes Ltd., on behalf of Andrea Plunket, Director of the Arthur Conan Doyle Trademark (EU).' For anyone interested in reading up on Jack the Ripper I found Paul Sugdon's *The Complete History of Jack the Ripper*, as well as *www.Casebook.org* to be of great value. I would like to thank all those who helped make this book possible: my publisher Steve Emecz, and Jon Lellenberg for introducing us; to Alice Smales for her editorial support; my readers, who kept me on the right path; Kate Pool at the Society of Authors for her invaluable assistance; Saunders Carmichael-Brown for dragging me singlehandedly into the 21st Century; and finally to my parents, for providing me with the support, patience and platform to write this book.

# PREFACE

IT IS WITH a heavy heart that I take up my pen and record what will be the first and indeed the last confession of Sherlock Holmes. It is a revelation so shocking in its nature, and so shameful in its bearing upon the public, that I am at considerable unease to reveal even my own minor role. For years I have wrestled with my conscience, danced with the demons in my mind: to be placed in a position of the utmost secrecy, while in possession of the facts regarding one of the most disturbing and infamous mysteries this country has ever known has been a terrible ordeal.

I have continued with my publications and scribed many more of Holmes's adventures but always I receive the same enquiries: I cannot satisfy their curiosity, I can offer no salvation. In matters of privacy, it is simple to hide accounts of delicacy, for they only require the consent and co-operation of a few individuals; but when an issue has been displayed before the world, this luxury is but a distant memory. No matter how much light is cast before the solitary wanderer, never can he resist the lure of the shadow. But now, at last, the world shall share my secret, and when they have experienced the horrors of the truth they shall wish to return to the blissful peace of mystery and wonderment.

I appeal directly to the heart and conscience of the individual, in the hope that, as they help alleviate me of this burden, they will not allow this darkest of episodes to tarnish any fond impression which they may have formulated regarding my dearest of friends, Sherlock Holmes.

# 1

# THE GREAT DUEL

IN THE YEAR of 1891, the capital of the British Empire was engulfed by the simmering clouds of civil war. For years this menace loomed over London like some form of vile arachnid slowly and meticulously descending upon its unsuspecting prey. Murder filled the streets, corruption poisoned the water, and at every turn the cornerstones of society were rife with decay. The very heart of the Empire was crumbling. Yet, remarkably, there was no retaliation. The Government were dismissive and the authorities perplexed. But, for Sherlock Holmes, this was the pinnacle of his career.

I had accompanied Holmes on many of his investigations but seldom did he seek my assistance during this most crucial of times. I had since departed bachelorhood and with it my room at Baker Street, having settled into lodgings and opened a private practice in Kensington with my wife Mary. We led a prosperous and content life, which was in stark contrast to the extremes that I had become accustomed to whilst living at 221B. I still continued to scour the papers for criminal reports containing any unusual features of interest, and as many of the public may recall, the first few months of that fateful year were notable due to the occurrence of several shocking murders.

In January, deep in the heart of that remorseless winter, a young couple, revered throughout the land for their generosity and charitable work for London's orphaned children, were found murdered, frozen in a pit of snow. Only their heads could be seen protruding from the pile; their faces only inches apart, as if they had been forced to watch their beloved slowly drift into oblivion. They were dressed in their evening attire, having attended a charity event earlier that evening in a nearby hotel. It was said that Mr. and Mrs. Ledger had no known quarrels, or even misunderstandings with anyone, and they were described as loving and energetic newlyweds who had dedicated their lives to the prosperity of London's misfortunate children.

The mystery caused a great outcry, as the press and public demanded answers from the authorities, but none could be found. The murders were ruthless, meticulously executed, yet completely unmotivated. Along with the rest of the civilised society, I remained horrified at these crimes and the apparent ease with which those responsible evaded even rumoured identification. It was therefore to further indignation that those seemingly responsible struck again the following month, when the body of Arthur Winchester, renowned entrepreneur and innovator of social housing reforms, was found floating lifelessly in the Thames.

The body was recovered on the riverbank near Fulham, having been dumped into the water a few miles North. Mr. Winchester had been severely beaten in the hours prior to his death before finally being stabbed shallowly in the vertebrae, and thrown into the water. The injuries were insufficient to kill the victim, and were believed to have been purposefully executed to prolong the man's suffering. Though Mr.Winchester likely had those in the world of business with whom he had not seen eye-to-eye, he was described as an amiable man, and one whose moral principles ensured that even the most stubborn of opposition held no qualm against him personally. Of course, certain landlords and developers were investigated as direct profiteers from Mr. Winchester's death, but once again, the police could find no satisfactory motive to the murder of a prominent, popular and progressive member of society.

Such a series of events is usually sufficient to send me upon my way to Baker Street: if not to offer my assistance, then to at least hear what would probably turn out to be the likely unravelling of the mystery from Holmes. Although he was never guaranteed to produce enough evidence to allow for a prosecution, at least I could find that certain sense of salvation and peace of mind which comes from a plausible understanding of the events, which helps anaesthetise the burning sense of injustice. Holmes, on the other hand, takes far more satisfaction in the knowledge that once again he has been able to unravel another intellectual puzzle.

Despite this, I had not had any correspondence with Holmes at all, save a couple of notes sent to me during his time spent in France while he was engaged by the French Government on a matter of supreme importance. Some may find this surprising for two great friends who live within reasonable walking distance of each other's doors. But such is the life of the world's only consulting detective that, on any occasion when I was free, he was often preoccupied or in a mood so undesirable that any visit would be instantly rendered pointless.

Happily, however, as winter's bitter grasp began to

relent under the gentle breeze of spring, I found ample time to visit Holmes, having wired ahead of my intentions. It was a bright yet brisk day, so I travelled by foot through Hyde Park. The sky was reflected perfectly in the Serpentine, and provided a pleasing imitation of warmer months.

I reached Baker Street around midday, rang the bell, and was greeted by dear Mrs. Hudson, a rather nanny-like woman, with a commendable nature and temperament. She is remarkable, particularly on account of her continuing relationship with Holmes, as I am certain there are few, if any, who would endure such a tenant.

Upon entering my old lodgings, I was instantly struck by the lack of light and a musty smell of stale neglect. It was clear that the two broad windows had remained firmly bolted for some days, and that Holmes had presumably spent that time skulking in the shadows. I had no intention of tolerating such conditions during my visit, so marched across to the window, and cast light and air back into the room. Holmes was not one for unnecessary change, and so it was no surprise to see that the sitting-room had remained cheerfully, yet practically furnished: a single sofa and two arm-chairs were the main focal point of the room, arranged around the large fireplace.

I decided against sitting in my old chair until Holmes had emerged from his quarters, and instead took a seat at the table, and lit my pipe. On top of a great pile of press-cuttings and other documents I found two pictures, both of which were instantly recognisable, and appeared to have been removed from their frames. The first was of a young, attractive couple; while the other was of a commanding man with a young boy, who was clearly the man's son. The pictures were of Mr. and Mrs.Ledger, and Arthur Winchester.

It was usual for Holmes to interest himself in such cases, but it did strike me as rather odd that he possessed two seemingly intimate pictures of the recently deceased. I did not recall his name being mentioned in the papers; and I was almost certain that he would have sought my assistance had he been engaged on such a case. My suspicions aroused, I continued to search through the pile before me, dusting off any of the fluffy ash of Arcadia which I spilt along the way, before coming across two quite unusual items. They both appeared to have been removed from the same small notebook. The first simply read 'Saturday, January 3rd, Gallery' and the second 'Friday, February 13th, Dockyard'.

'I see you have made yourself at home once again, Watson,' said Sherlock Holmes, finally emerging from his bedroom.

I began to smile at the realisation that he had fully intended for me to see such data; but, as I glanced up, I was almost thrown from my chair, such was the shock that greeted me. His usual sharply defined, hawk-like features, were becoming increasingly transparent, as if he were being dragged into a lifeless purgatory.

'Good God, Holmes, you look awful! What on earth has happened to you?'

'I am engaged on a case.'

'Which requires that you do not eat, leave your rooms, and remain constantly in the dark?'

'It is not essential, only advisable.'

'But what could possibly require such action?'

'I believe you know the answer, my dear fellow, you just do not wish to admit it,' he said, glancing down at the photographs.

I admit that I was rather disturbed by Holmes. His mannerisms, which were often eccentric and unpredictable, had come to resemble those of a desolate soul upon being admitted into a sanatorium. Never had I seen him so haggard.

'You knowwho is responsible for these crimes?'

'Naturally,' he replied casually.

'Who?'

'Is there no name which springs to mind?'

'Moriarty?'

'I once told you that he is the instigator of almost all that is evil in our great city. Well, there is your proof,' said he, pointing to the photographs, before flinging himself onto the sofa. 'He has a mind of the highest calibre; in fact I would go as far as to say, it is no exaggeration that I have met my true intellectual equal. He organises virtually all undetected crime, leaving but a hollow strand of evidence. For years I have felt this power, this disturbance in the commonplace criminal equilibrium: robberies, corruption, murders, I have investigated a wealth of crime where, though I could not prove it so, I knew that the true perpetrator had not been brought to justice. It is maddening, Watson! To see these terrible injuries: young, innocent lives, torn and tortured, while the hand that guides the knife remains completely anonymous. These cases, people say there is no motive. *I* am the motive! The dates and events you see were sent to me by Moriarty, a warning, that if I continue to thwart his designs, more people will die, before eventually he will turn his entire focus upon me. It has taken me three years to weave my way into the great spider's web, but only now, after a great game, am I close to the belly of the beast.'

'Is there nothing you can do?'

'I have gone too far to turn back.'

'But how many more will die?'

'At least one.'

'How can you be so sure?'

'I received this three days ago in the morning post,' he said, passing me a slip of paper. Upon it were the words, 'April, Tuesday 21st, Westminster'. 'What you are examining Watson, is Moriarty's idea of a game: for every inconvenience I cause him, he retaliates with a public and brutal murder, of some of our finest and most beloved citizens. Previously such information was sent to me after the murders, a perverse bill of sale, if you will. This time, though, my crime has been acknowledged in advance, and I am forced to await the consequences. I have been waiting for Inspector Patterson to call upon Baker Street ever since.'

'But why haven't you moved to protect these people?'

'Tell me who is to be next, and I shall act.'

'But how could I possibly know that?'

'I may ask you that exact same question.'

'But have there been no clues, no small piece of minutiae for you to follow?'

'If Moriarty wanted to send me on a wild chase throughout the City, he is well within his power to do so. But I am afraid he finds it far more enjoyable to offer me no such opportunity, and instead prefers to give me the option to act, and then send me pictures of those who I have allowed to die.'

'Surely you do not blame yourself for these murders, Holmes? You have been left with no alternative.'

'For now, Watson, you are right. But I would draw my career to a close this very hour if only I could be assured of freeing the public of such a dangerous antagonist.'

Before I could ask Holmes quite what he meant by this rather ominous remark, I was interrupted by the ringing of the bell, and then the sound of hurried, heavy boots upon the stairs. A moment later the door flew open and

Inspector Paterson came marching into the room. He was a large, powerful man with hair so red he would have been an ideal candidate for the Red-Headed League. His features were hard, but there was something in his light blue eyes, which suggested this was also a man capable of deep thought and humility.

'There has been another murder, Inspector?' asked Holmes, rising to his feet.

'Not murder, Mr. Holmes, but suicide. Mr. Robert Snetterton was found earlier, dead at his desk.'

'The MP?' I asked, dumbfounded.

Robert Snetterton was an up and coming Radical, a charismatic and most gifted young politician whose work toward Liberal reform was second to none, and he was already being tipped as a future Home Secretary and even Prime Minister. Though the previous victims had been tragic, the potential murder of a prominent politician went beyond anything that Moriarty had previously executed.

'Unfortunately yes,' replied Patterson. 'However, it may interest you, Mr. Holmes, to know that although there was poison in Snetterton's whisky, only one vial could be found on the premises, unopened upon his desk; and despite the note which he wrote, there appears to be no motive for such action. We have managed to keep word from spreading, but that will not last forever. I am sure you appreciate the delicacy of the situation, Mr. Holmes, and I need you to come right away. You too, Dr. Watson, if Mr. Holmes desires it.'

'I certainly do,' said Holmes, reaching for his coat.

We immediately set off for Charlwood Street, and were fortunate that the streets were rather quiet, arriving at our destination in good time. Mr. Snetterton lived in a well-to-do neighbourhood, and his house, as were the rest on the street, was of Georgian origin, well-kept and modest. We exited our cab, and set off down the short path, before being ushered up the steps and across the threshold by Inspector Patterson. We found ourselves in a relatively narrow corridor with closed doors upon each side.

'Mr. Snetterton has a servant,' stated Holmes, examining the door which led to the servant's quarters. 'Was he in the house at the time of death?'

'No; he had received word that morning that his mother had been struck gravely ill, and had set off immediately. He found the body upon his return, and he claimed Mr.Snetterton had mentioned nothing of guests before.'

'Ha, we shall soon see about that,' said Holmes.

In a matter of moments, he had closely examined the path, the door through which we just entered, the floor and the all the doorways along the corridor, before finally pausing with a most perplexed look upon his brow. Clearly dissatisfied, he opened the door at the end of the corridor, and entered into what was presumably Snetterton's study.

Inspector Patterson and I soon joined Holmes in the room, which was spacious and tastefully decorated. We found Mr. Snetterton slumped across a large oak desk, his face terribly contorted, and a glass of whisky spilt before him across a great array of papers. There was a single large window behind him that looked out across the garden and illuminated the room, which Holmes examined first, but to no success. He then examined the body from a variety of angles; satisfied, he turned his attention to the whisky, sniffing it with his hound-like nose. He then crossed the room to a large wooden drinks cabinet, removed a full decanter and inhaled deeply. Finally, he came back to the desk, picking up the suicide note, along with another of the many sheets which were indiscriminately spread across the desk.

'There has been no sign of forcible entry anywhere in this house,' he said. 'His murderer must have been known to him.'

'But how could he have been murdered?' asked Patterson, bemused. 'You hold in your hand the note which Snetterton wrote before he consumed the poison, and you said so yourself, there is no evidence of anyone forcibly entering this building.'

'The whisky in Snetterton's glass is not the same as that found in the decanter in his drinks cabinet, and the vial of poison on the desk is, as you have rightly stated, unopened. As for the note, Snetterton did not write it,' said Holmes, passing him the document. 'The words are rather convincing, so your mistake is understandable, but if you examine it alongside another piece of Snetterton's writing, you will notice that the upward stroke upon the letter 'G' is irregular, and that the 'S' has a slightly uncharacteristic flourish.'

'My word, you are right!' exclaimed Patterson. 'But if it wasn't suicide, who killed him?'

'It was a well-educated man of respectable class; he is exceedingly tall and thin, with a domed forehead, and two deep-set sunken eyes. His shoulders are rounded, and he has a pale, clean shaven face which protrudes forward.'

'How in God's name did you come up with all that? You cannot tell me such information can be conjured from a man's handwriting!' exclaimed Patterson.

'Simple, Inspector. The murderer's name is Professor James Moriarty.'

'Moriarty? You believe Snetterton was part of this criminal empire we have been tracking?'

'No, I do not. You are forgetting, Inspector, that to general society Moriarty is a revered and celebrated academic and mathematician, not the Napoleon of crime which we know him to be. Snetterton would have been completely unaware of just who he had welcomed warmly into his home.'

'But how can you be sure it was him?'

'You are of course aware of my investigations, Inspector, but I have not informed you how these recent murderers are related.'

'Murders? There has been more than one?'

'Robert Snetterton, Arthur Winchester, and Mr. and Mrs. Ledger, were all murdered by Professor Moriarty.'

'But how do you know all this?'

'I have been sent tokens after each of our successes in which we have thwarted Moriarty. Three days ago, I received another such receipt for our work, and have since been waiting for you to contact me. I did not divulge such information, as I was worried you would not wish to continue. Now though, I believe I have formulated a sufficient case to end this ordeal once and for all.'

'You *knew* that someone was going to die,' said Patterson furiously, taking a step towards Holmes, 'and you didn't tell me?'

'Had I informed you of such events, you may have been much less enthusiastic in assisting me against Moriarty; and I assure you Inspector, that unfortunate though these murders are, they are inconsequential if we are successful in bringing an end to the Professor. I had no way of knowing *who* would die; and nor could I have been certain that this was the murder I had been expecting until I came and examined the scene. You asked for my help, so here it is: Mr. Snetterton welcomed Professor Moriarty into his home with open arms; Moriarty brought with him a particularly fine bottle of whisky, and offered his host a toast, which he happily accepted. If you need any further assurances, the poison found in the unopened vial would have offered a far more preferable death than the cruel drawn-out fate Snetterton suffered. No sane man would opt for such an unpleasant end. Moriarty watched the man die, placed the fabricated note upon the desk, and left with the real poison.'

'But all the evidence points to suicide. I cannot arrest Moriarty based upon assumption! What will I say in my reports and to the press?'

'Burn the note, and remove the vial of poison; report that Snetterton's death was accidental, caused by an unnatural reaction to a usually harmless chemical which was found in his drink. The lack of motive, forcible entry and fatal reaction to what is often an innocuous substance should be enough to satisfy those of any wrong-doing.'

'Are you mad?' Patterson cried.

'I am afraid that a completely unmotivated suicide will not be accepted, and a further inquest will ensue, which, given time, will conclude it must have been murder. Moriarty desires this back-lash, Inspector: it is the next step in his design. You must act how you see fit, but I can only assure you that we shall have our man soon enough. We will not be able to convict him of all these crimes, but we at least shall know the culprit has been brought to justice.'

Having left Charlwood Street, Holmes returned to Baker Street, and I to Kensington, where to my great disappointment, I learnt that Mary had been urgently requested by her old employer and friend, Mrs. Cecil Forrester, and had departed immediately. I therefore dined at my old club, and played numerous rounds of cards before returning to my lodgings and the latest edition of the Medical Journal, with a cigar and glass of brandy. It was deep into the evening and my mind had begun to drift: I was aware of reading the words before me, but I failed to extract any meaning from them.

'Now is not the time for rest, Watson,' said Sherlock Holmes, emerging unannounced from the doorway.

'Holmes!' I cried, spilling my drink as I jolted awake.

'I apologise for my imprudence,' he said, with a minor chuckle at my misfortune, pouring himself a drink and then refilling my own. 'But I assure you it was impossible for me to wait at your door. I have been hounded almost every step since we departed.'

'What on earth has happened to you?'

'After the cab dropped you off I journeyed back to Baker Street with the full intention of dining and continuing my plan of action regarding Moriarty. You can imagine then, what a great surprise it was when I entered my lodgings to find the very man who had consumed my thoughts sitting upon the sofa, awaiting my arrival. I consider myself master of all my faculties, as you know, but even I confess to feeling a slight thrill of fear shudder down my spine. Never have I encountered a man with such a callous and unforgiving nature.

'You are late,' said he, both hands resting upon a heavy, wooden cane.

'I was unaware that I would be entertaining guests, otherwise I would have ensured I was here to welcome you upon arrival,' I said, shutting the door and walking across the room to my desk.

'Your reputation appears to be unwarranted, Mr. Holmes: a man of your intellect should know better than to assume that I would not have removed the firearm from your desk. Do you really consider me so uncivilised?'

'I have witnessed your work, Professor,' I said, turning from the desk and taking a seat opposite my guest. 'And I assure you that I would not slander your ability with the label of uncivilised.'

'You flatter me; but I am afraid that compliments and my admiration for your skill are at an end' said he, consulting a small leather-bound notebook. 'The situation has become an impossible one, Mr. Holmes. Through your continual persecution I have found my plans increasingly frustrated to such a degree that I am now in danger of losing my liberty.'

'What do you suggest?' I enquired.

'You must stop playing this game,' he said, his gaze boring into my eyes with a fierce intensity.

'Surely Professor, you know that I cannot stop playing until the game has reached its natural conclusion. As a dedicated player one must have respect for the rules and traditions of the sport; I could never simply abandon the match.'

'You place me in a very inconvenient position; a man of your stature will surely deduce that there can be only one outcome. Observing the way in which you have wrestled with this affair has been a great pleasure; you are perhaps the one man who can satisfy me intellectually. It would grieve me to have to take matters into my own hands. You may smile, but I speak truthfully. For too long I was unopposed, unrivalled in my profession. Even when I publicly flaunted my faculty, still those mindless dogs could not even manage a sniff!'

'The dogs may have been chasing their tails, but I assure you I got far more than a *sniff*.'

'That may be so,' he replied, with a slight stutter of discomposure.

'If there is nothing more of any real concern, Professor, I must insist, my time is most valuable.'

'It seems a pity,' said he, rising from his chair. 'I have done what I could. It has been a great duel between you and I, Mr. Holmes. If you are clever enough to bring destruction upon me, then rest assured that I should do as much to you.'

'You have paid me several compliments, Mr. Moriarty, so let me pay you one in return; when I say that if I were assured of the former eventuality, I would cheerfully accept the latter.'

'In response, the Professor simply smiled at me with, I admit, a most unnerving expression, before placing a photograph on the table and swiftly making his exit.'

'What an extraordinary encounter,' I said. 'I assume the photograph was of Robert Snetterton?'

'Indeed it was; the audacity of Moriarty is quite intolerable. I had only been turning over recent events in my mind for a short while before I was alarmed by the smell of smoke. The ceiling of the apartment below had rather inconveniently caught fire, and was now spreading into my quarters. Fortunately, Mrs. Hudson and myself emerged unscathed, and nothing of value was lost. Having assured that she was safe and of a sound frame of mind, I decided to leave Baker Street. I had not been wandering for five minutes when I was almost run down by a particularly reckless two-horse van. I avoided disaster by a whisker, and stuck to the pavements, only to find myself inches away from being struck by a fallen brick from the roof above. Certain this was no accident, I increased my pace and carried on toward Pall Mall and my brother Mycroft's lodgings, where I spent the rest of the day. I waited for the cover of darkness before journeying here but was attacked by a rough, armed with a bludgeon. I left him in a rather unenviable condition in the street for a patrolling constable to find. But again, there was no proof linking this man to the esteemed Professor. So you see, Watson, that despite my every precaution, I am still being ruthlessly hunted, and it is for this reason that I must ask whether you are prepared to accompany me to the Continent?'

'Straightaway?'

'Tomorrow morning.'

'I have an accommodating neighbour, and fortunately Mary is away upon a visit, of course I shall accompany you.'

'Mary is with Mycroft.'

'I beg your pardon?'

'I presented her with a set of instructions to ensure that there was no suggestion of her having gone anywhere but to see her old Governess. She is in fact at Pall Mall under Mycroft's protection.'

'Well, I appreciate your efforts, Holmes, but was this really necessary?'

'Every precaution is necessary when you are dealing with Moriarty. You have seen what he is capable of; he would not hesitate to do the same to Mary. Now to business,' he said, leaning forwards. 'You will need to carry out my instructions precisely Watson or we should find ourselves at the bottom of the Channel, instead of sailing merrily over it.'

~

The following morning I followed the exact and elaborate design Holmes had instructed me with in order to safely reach the Continental train at Victoria. Fortunate I am to have such an ally, for if I had not been given such instructions, I would have surely met with a most unpleasant end. As instructed, I sent my man to send for a hansom, ignoring the first two, and then wasted no time jumping into the third, urging haste, whilst brandishing a slip of paper to the driver for the Strand end of Lowther Arcade. It was only a matter of seconds before Moriarty's men were upon our tail, desperately attempting to keep pace. My driver, likely hand-chosen by Holmes himself, whipped the steeds into action, forging a path through the unsuspecting traffic. Our pursuers, though inconvenienced by the resulting mêlée of horses and carriages, were unfazed by such obstacles, impossibly carving a passage with frightful ease. I had my fare ready, and tossed it to the cabbie before he drew to a halt, as the sharp whistle of bullets suddenly caused an explosion of splinters behind me. I leapt from the carriage, weaving amongst the traffic, and narrowly avoiding a particularly eager cabbie. I dashed through the Arcade, aware of the pursuers still hot upon my heels. Again I owed myself to Holmes's keen sense of preparation, for not a moment had passed before I leapt into the waiting brougham, than I saw the murderous stare of my momentarily defeated opponents. I kept my revolver at hand and maintained a vigilant guard until we reached the relative safety of Victoria.

Exiting my carriage I scoured the area for any sign of danger, for it was abundantly clear from my assault that Moriarty was no longer concerned about discretion.

As I entered the station it did not take long to find my luggage, which had been sent on unaddressed the previous evening. Holmes had reserved us a first-class carriage, the only one marked 'engaged.' My only source of apprehension was that Sherlock Holmes had yet to appear. The station clock ticked ever closer to our departure, so I decided to search amongst the travellers for my elusive friend. I took no comfort in the knowledge that my pursuers were nowhere to be seen: for if they were no longer preoccupied with me, they must be hounding Holmes's every step. I waited until the last possible moment before accepting the futility of my plight, and returned worriedly to my seat. I had no choice but to trust in the powers Holmes had so often demonstrated, and now that Moriarty was upon my track, I could not stay in London; I had to remain confident that even with such a daunting pursuer, Holmes would eventually join me at some stage of the journey.

Incapable of freeing myself from anxiety, I stared out of the window, often straining to look down the carriage, as if expecting to see Holmes impossibly clinging to the outside of the train with a glint of triumph in his eye. My rather fanciful delusion went unfulfilled, so I reluctantly took my seat in the dining carriage. I did not have the stomach for breakfast, and the usual calming effects of morning tea were insufficient in alleviating me of my apprehension. Rather unsatisfied, I returned to my carriage, only to find that my privacy had been invaded by a thoroughly unkempt Italian priest, whose command of the English language was, to my surprise, inferior even to my Italian. Alas, I soon realised any attempt to educate my new companion upon the ways of the English class system was futile, and such was my boredom I found myself briefly lecturing him on Fredk W. Burton's latest work upon the *Putrefactive Decomposition In The Intestinal Tract*. Though giving me cause for momentary distraction, my educative desires waned, and I found myself drifting back into the steady, monotonous bumps of our great rail network, before being startled by a most familiar voice.

'Though I appreciate your attempts to enlighten me upon the way in which poisonous bodies derived from our food pass along the alimentary tract, Watson, I am still rather insulted to find you in such a state of relaxation. But not to worry, our connection at Canterbury is in five minutes.'

I had seen my great friend transform himself on many

occasions but the apparent ease which he achieved this feat still astounded me: the previously wrinkled skin; the natural droop of features tired from the everlasting battle against time; the slightly protruding and quivering top lip, all disappeared to reveal the exhausted, yet jubilant, apparition of Sherlock Holmes.

'I assure you, Holmes, I have not enjoyed a single moment of my journey,' said I, indignantly. 'Being hounded and fired upon by Moriarty's men is hardly a desirable start to the day. But may I enquire as to why we are no longer boarding the ferry at Dover?'

'For the simple reason that I wish to avoid a mortal attack at the hands of Professor Moriarty; it took some ingenuity and a large slice of luck, but I was just able to give our friend the slip before boarding the train. I was in such a state of triumph that I confess, I had entirely forgotten that our agreed upon rendezvous was in fact this very carriage.'

'But if you managed to escape Moriarty, why must we depart at Canterbury? Surely we shall be safe upon the ferry.'

'No Watson, Moriarty will not give up the hunt so hastily. If I were in his predicament, I would simply engage a special; the delay at both Canterbury and Dover will provide ample time for him to catch us. We must always assume that he also would take such action.'

Unfortunately our connection at Canterbury was delayed, and we found ourselves waiting upon the platform. We had been stationary for only a matter of moments, when Holmes pulled at my sleeve, pointing up the line, and urging me to take refuge behind a pile of luggage. In the distance, a thin tower of smoke began to emerge from the faraway trees, and we saw an engine with a single carriage, hurtling toward the English coastline. It was only a matter of seconds after we had taken refuge that we felt the hot blaze of burning coal and murderous intent sear past our faces.

'Now Watson, we must make haste for Newhaven, where, if we arrive in sufficient time, we may find ourselves with the luxury of enjoying a spot of lunch.'

~

In comparison to our escape, the first few days of our brief excursion abroad were most enjoyable. Having spent two days in Brussels, we spent our third in Strasburg, where, to my utmost pleasure even Holmes began to enjoy himself. That is until he read the reply to his morning's telegraph to London.

'Moriarty has escaped,' said he with a heated air of frustration in his voice. 'I made the mistake in believing anyone other than myself could bring him in, and now I am afraid it has not only ruined my plan, but also, dear Watson, our holiday. You must return to England.'

'You are perhaps a little angered by what has taken place, Holmes, but do not allow that to cloud your judgment over my loyalty,' I said devoutly.

'I could not possibly ask such a task of you. The Professor's game is up, my dear fellow, and you must realise the danger we are both now in.'

Eventually Holmes realised that I could not be swayed, and I believe that he was, in his own way, grateful for my company. No man wishes to tread the path of eternity alone, even if they stray back onto the edge of mortality. We therefore continued with our travels, following our feet up the Valley of the Rhone, before detouring via Leuk and over the Gemmi Pass. An idealist would have failed to choose a more serene and idyllic route for our journey. The elegant grace of the spring valleys, complimented dazzling whites of the mountain peaks, was an ... such comforting beauty that any man would contemplate it as his last. Try as I would to encourage Holmes to absorb our surroundings, his focus would not be ... Vigilance of the highest order was meticulously ... Each passing face, no matter how commonplace, ... met with a piercing gaze of fierce scrutiny, and I noticed how victims sharply increased their pace. On more than one occasion, a large rock came crashing down, narrowly missing us. With startling ease over such terrain, Holmes would be upon the summit of the ridge before the boulder lost its velocity, always returning with a glint of ... in his eye. Even amongst the well-trodden paths, ... found hints of our dogged pursuer.

'You see, Watson,' said he, delicately poised ... of prints in the snow. 'These are the tracks ... particular pair of shoes: hand-crafted person... John Lobb, for Professor Moriarty. I observed ... such a pair upon his visit to Baker Street: th... shape are identical, while the indent in the s... the height of the heel to that of the Profess... also notice that these prints are always tr... larger set. Moriarty is trying his utmost t... tracks.'

'But how can you be sure of your conclusi... I replied. 'Could the tracks not simply have ... a taller man with a larger foot than Moriart...

'If you observe, all will unfold. Take not... the larger print, as well as the length of the s... we observe the secondary print, its rela... position within the larger is quite clearly out... It is possible, of course, that Moriarty is tr... us off the scent, but owing to his burning ...

destruction upon me', I wo... r such a hypothesis highly unlikely.'

'You ...elive Moria... rought a brigade of henchme... upn the Con?'... nd they are travelling in single fil... de their ... ny, I believe he has only

'No, ...tsn; unfo... brought ...re, thoug... ou correctly deduce, they are undoubt... travellin... single file. Moriarty would not prematu...sk his... osure by naively relying upon orchestr... smal... attalion. It is most likely that he has brou... hi... his most capable of servants, Colonel Sebastia...'

Mor...most distinctly unpleasant individual. Consid...ngst military circles as one of the top marksn...ope, he was deemed too dangerous for the Brit...n India, and upon his return to London continu... an evil reputation. His talents did not go unn...oriarty. After a short period of service Moran ...promoted as Moriarty's Chief-of-Staff, and w...pon only for jobs of the utmost import...or this reason that Holmes referred to him a... most dangerous man in London.' Until ... my nerves had been steady; I had believe...s and I were a match for any pursuer, but su...ation of Moran that I could not help but fee...er of fear. I was sure we continued to draw ...ause Moriarty wished to personally murde... cold blood.

De...ting pursuers, Holmes insisted we contin...ey, soon passing through Interlaken and a...illage of Meiringen on the third of May. ...mmodation for the night at a small hotel ...lishcher Hof, whose owner, Peter Steile...ke fluent English, having waited tables at the Grosvenor Hotel in London for three years. It was his advice that, having rested comfortably, Holmes and I should visit the hamlet of Rosenlaui; but also that under no circumstances should we pass up the opportunity of a visit to the falls of Reichenbach along the way.

Never have I laid eyes upon such terrifying beauty. The cascading torrent burst over the inadequate lip as the relentless waves plunged into a void of jagged, coal-black rock: the merciless entrance to an eternal chasm. Deep from within the depths of this perpetual abyss arose great towers of spray, encompassing the grand fortification. As Holmes and I gazed into this ominous, yet mesmerising feat of nature, we listened to the faceless haunting choir, echoing from the elusive chamber from within the very heart of the fall: a perverse serenade of enticing malevolence. We found ourselves bewitched by the tantalising charm, and so followed the path which led into the falls itself before finding that our route abruptly terminated halfway round. Having spent ample time admiring the falls, we turned to continue our day's journey on toward Rosenlaui, when we were approached by a young Swiss boy. He arrived in a state of exhaustion, tightly clutching a letter addressed to me and bearing our hotel's crest. It was an urgent plea from our landlord; an Englishwoman travelling from Davos Platz to Lucerne had been struck by a sudden haemorrhage as she had made to leave our hotel. He did not believe that she had many remaining hours, and said that it would be a great comfort for her to see an English doctor.

'You must go, Watson,' said Sherlock Holmes, eyes transfixed on the abyss below, 'you cannot deny an English lady upon her death-bed.'

'But Holmes, by the time I descend the path back to

the hotel, she will either have passed on or be in such a condition as to render my presence obsolete. She would be completely incapable of acknowledging such a gesture.'

'You are of course sensible in your conclusions, Watson, but would you, of all people, be able to look yourself in the eye having known that you neglected your duty? If Mary was in such a position, would you not wish her to be eased into the afterlife, no matter how trivial the comfort?'

It was most unlike Holmes to offer such an argument. Never before had I heard him place emotional sentiment before the cold, hard reasoning of logic.

'I will leave your side, Holmes, only if the boy accompanies you to Rosenlaui. I, of course, cannot deny a woman's dying wish, but I refuse to leave you without a companion.'

'I have no qualms with such a course of action,' said Holmes. 'I shall remain here for a little while longer, but then we shall progress toward our inn for the night.'

I left Holmes leaning against the rock-face, arms folded, gazing into the fall. I made haste away from Reichenbach, not wishing to leave Holmes any longer than was necessary. When I approached the bottom of my descent, I turned back for a fleeting glance at my old friend, but my feet had carried me too far. Upon the one-way path above, still visible from my position, I noted the silhouette of a man walking at a great and purposeful pace; but such was my haste to reach the poor dying woman that I cast this image from my mind, a feat in later years I found myself unable to replicate. I reached the hotel in little over an hour; the landlord was seated upon his porch-chair, smoking contently in the late-afternoon sun.

'How is the patient?' said I, surprised at his lackadaisical appearance upon my approach.

It was the flicker of the man's bemused expression however, which caused me to stop in my tracks. 'Who wrote this?' said I, brandishing the letter before his eyes. 'Where is the dying Englishwoman?'

'There has not been an Englishwoman here for weeks!' he cried. 'Though that is the hotel mark, it must have been that tall Englishman who came in minutes after your departure.' There was no doubt in my mind as to the identity of this mysterious man. Without awaiting further explanation, I turned and fled in a state of fear that cut down to my very soul. On countless occasions in Afghanistan I had run toward the face of death, but the journey I now faced required an entirely different form of courage.

Desperate though I was, it was a full two hours before I arrived back onto the narrow path. I reached the rock where I had left Holmes staring out into the distance; only his Alpine-stock remained, perched against the cliff face. There was no sign of Holmes.

I went to the edge of the fall and called out desperately over the roar. I received no reply, only the echo of my own pleas against the unforgiving howl of the waters. For a moment, I could do nothing but stare lifelessly into the abyss, my mind refusing to comprehend the conclusions which I knew to be true. The torrents continued to crash down before me, relentlessly torturing me with the vision of how my greatest of friends had been dragged and torn away into the merciless mist.

I took a moment to gather myself beforeturning my attention to the task at hand. It was Holmes's Alpine-stock which turned my heart cold; he had not carried on to Rosenlaui. He had awaited his pursuer upon the three-foot path, trapped between an insurmountable rock-face and a perilous drop. The young Swiss lad had disappeared: I am certain he was in the pay of Moriarty.

I journeyed beyond the rock where I last laid eyes upon Holmes and found, deeply imbedded into the ceaselessly damp black soil, two sets of unmistakable footprints leading directly toward the edge of the fall. Neither had returned. I went to the end of the path, past the thorns which encircled the chasm, and lay down in the mud, my face peering out over the edge, penetrating the periphery of one of the great towers of spray. My efforts were futile. My ears were once again pounded by the half-human cry of the falls, as my eyes failed to see anything in the impenetrable darkness.

As I wandered in hopelessness back toward his Alpine-stock, I discovered two distinct traces of tobacco ash, and was rather shocked to conclude that the two great rivals had enjoyed one last cigarette together. I stood and contemplated Holmes's rather singular frame of mind, and could not help but be in a confused awe of his character. I picked up his belongings and turned to leave; but such is the nature of my great friend, I was destined to hear from him one last time.

From a nearby boulder came an unnatural glint of light, and raising my hand, I discovered the source was Holmes's silver cigarette case. I intended to slip this token into my pocket and depart as readily as possible, but a small square of paper glided to the ground and stopped me in my tracks. Unfolding it, I discovered it was three pages torn from Holmes's notebook. The dictation was clear, calm and precise. He may well have been writing from his study.

'My dear Watson,' said he. 'I write these few lines through the courtesy of Mr. Moriarty, who awaits my convenience for the final discussion of those questions which lie between us. He has been giving me a sketch of the methods by which he avoided the English police and kept himself informed of our movements. They certainly confirm the very high opinion which I had formed of his abilities. I am pleased to think that I shall be able to free society of his presence, though I fear that it is at a cost which will give pain to my friends, and especially, my dear Watson, to you. I have already explained to you, however, that my career had reached its crisis, and that no possible conclusion to it could be more congenial to me than this. Indeed, if I may make a full confession to you, I was quite convinced that the letter from Meiringen was a hoax, and I allowed you to depart on that errand under the persuasion that some development of this sort would follow. Tell Inspector Patterson that the papers which he needs to convict the gang are in pigeon-hole M., done up in a blue envelope and inscribed 'Moriarty'. I made every disposition of my property before leaving England, and handed it to my brother Mycroft. Pray give my greetings to Mrs. Watson, and believe me to be, my dear fellow,

Very sincerely yours,
Sherlock Holmes.

A few words may suffice to tell the little that remains. An examination by experts leaves little doubt that a personal contest between the two men ended, as it could hardly fail to end in such a situation, in their reeling over, locked in each others arms. Any attempt at recovering the bodies was absolutely hopeless, and there deep down in that dreadful cauldron of swirling water and seething foam, will lie for all time the most dangerous criminal and the foremost champion of the law of their generation.

# 2

# A MOST SINGULAR OCCURRENCE

FOR YEARS I have tried to fill that void in my life: to turn hollow words back into poetry, the endless droning of orchestras into soft melodies. A bellowing silence grasped the Continent, which still bore the deep invisible scars of the conflict which had taken place between the late Sherlock Holmes and Professor James Moriarty. A great state of mourning had seemingly descended across every nation, yet none appeared aware of the cause behind their sombre disposition. I took to travelling upon the Continent in the hope of discovering some form of salvation. I cannot recall how much time I spent lifelessly drifting from country to country: I could muster no admiration of Vienna; no love or sentiment for the great stream of bridges and waterways in Venice; no sense of grandeur in Rome. All I could see were petty thieves, incapable roughs and despicable orchestrators.

I often mused to myself which I considered more hateful: a public under the control of Moriarty, or under the brutish control of the inept. For what seemed like an age, I considered the similarities to be found amongst Europe's criminally mundane, but it was not until I engaged in the study of the faculty that I truly appreciated the outstanding. Although Sherlock Holmes was no longer able to demonstrate those powers which so often astounded me, I decided to imitate his methods to broaden my understandings of the criminal mentality: I observed, I analysed and I deduced the subtleties which set certain crimes apart. Most, of course, were quite un-extraordinary; their lack of imagination and craft merely reflected the tedious routine of the authorities. Both factions had ostensibly agreed to enter into some form of uneasy armistice; neither had the guile or the craftsmanship to continue the struggle which had consumed the lives of the two great adversaries.

Though I had always admired Holmes' abilities, I could not help but be struck by the brilliance of *Moriarty*. To weave such a web, to build such an empire out of almost completely hapless material was an achievement of the ages. As I delved further into the underworld, I wandered in horror as his successors tarnished his once-great empire with their shameful banality.

I therefore decided to honour the legacy of both men by the best means at my disposal. I made it my purpose to demonstrate the incompetence of both the criminal and the authorities. Why simply rob a person when you can manipulate them: toy with their emotions and find a way to incriminate *them*. Why must the criminal always be the villain? Perhaps now that I have rebalanced the scales and left the official-forces perplexed in so many of Europe's great countries, they will finally bow to the wisdom of Sherlock Holmes and seek to broaden their tragically narrow horizons.

It was in the dawn of 1894 that I found myself embroiled in a case of particular intrigue. My travels had taken me to Montpellier, the capital of the Languedoc-Roussillon region in southern France. It was here,whilst enjoying light refreshment after a visit to the Cathédrale St-Pierre, that I had the misfortune to be introduced to a most ghastly gentleman, Henri de Saint-Hippolyte. His expression was keen yet dim, and his handsome features were somewhat diminished due to the blandness of their regularity. It soon became apparent that he possessed neither talent nor intellect; I have found more charm even from those hopelessly pretentious and insufferable fools found haunting the boulevards of Paris. But, despite my insistence upon the matter, he refused to leave me until I had accepted an invitation to dine at his estate on Friday evening.

I could imagine no more dismal an affair, and had no intention of fulfilling such a commitment; that is, until I discovered that Monsieur de Saint-Hippolyte was soon expected to inherit a rather fine collection of *objets de vertu.* Such were the rumours surrounding this collection that I concluded that they were at least worthy of inspection, and though dreading the evening's events, I was at least pleasantly reminded of my fondness of dressing for such occasions. It had been a considerable time since I had allowed myself the indulgence of formal affairs.

I took a carriage from my lodgings and noted the disgruntled look upon the driver's face as I gave him my destination. After a relatively brief journey, I found myself travelling through a great archway of trees, the moonlight shining through the steady swaying of the bare branches providing me with a dance of shadow and graceful percussion. I was entertained by this performance of rhythm and silhouette for a considerable time before arriving at the entrance to a grand house. It was an impressive sight, but served only to increase my contempt for Monsieur de Saint-Hippolyte; who, to my surprise, welcomed me himself.

'Madam, even our most beautiful of regions pale in comparison to your elegance,' said he, taking my hand. 'I do not believe I have ever seen such beauty.'

'You are most kind, Monsieur de Saint-Hippolyte.'

'Ah please, Henri.'

'Very well, Henri. You have a truly remarkable home; rarely have I seen such magnificence. If you would be so kind, perhaps later in the evening I could have the grand tour? Unless of course you are busy with your *other* guests.'

'Of course not, my flower. I am sure we can slip away for a time, but first we must at least *appear* to be sociable. Please, come this way and meet my guests.'

I can scarcely recall a more tortuous endeavour. I have been guest to many such occasions, but never had I the misfortune to suffer such company. Arrogant men with their tales of prosperity, conveniently ignoring how they owed their entire livelihood to their fathers; cackling women who married into such lives purely because they have no other worthwhile gifts themselves, other than weak and often insufficient attempts at benevolence.

It is fortunate that most men are such simple animals: as little as a dainty smile, a quick glance, or the batting of an eyelid is sufficient to turn their customary stonewall guards instantly to dust. It was therefore with relative ease that, after the formalities of dining and entertaining had been attended too, I managed to pry Henri away from his guests and procure the previously agreed upon tour.

As we travelled down the many passageways, I glided

along with flirtatious grace, and occasionally allowed a suggestive, yet subtly accidental brush of finger upon glove. One day men may learn to guard themselves against such behaviour, for upon my gentle insistence I viewed every downstairs room. Fortunately, I did not have to worry myself with any excuse for abstaining from a tour of the upstairs: such a course of action would have been most improper. The undeniable evidence of prints in dust was the only complication which I would have to contend with, for each adequate escape route was covered in the powder of the burglar's downfall.

'Henri,' said I, in a sickeningly soft sweet tone. 'I have heard such *wonderful* things about your Aunt's collection, and it would be such an awful omission to miss it, having admired the rest of your home. May we see it before the night is through?'

'We shall see it soon enough, my dear,' said he, a slightly surprised, though predictably satisfied resonance to his tone. 'We must wait for her to retire first.'

I must confess that I was rather taken by the splendour of the *objets de vertu*; such was the contrast between possession and likely inheritor that it was clear the apple had indeed fallen very far from the tree. The pride of the collection was a chased-gold snuffbox, crafted by the fabulous Jean Ducrollay, intricately enamelled in the style of a fanned peacock's tail. To the annoyance of my host, however, I was not infatuated by his most prized possession, but by the startling beauty of a gold, Parisian bodice ornament. I was instantly mesmerised by five rose-cut diamonds, accompanied by the further five drops of the bow pendant: its elegance accentuated its modesty. There was also a pair of girandole earrings, styled in the form of a bow, both with three drops decorated with faceted point-cut diamonds, which sparkled irresistibly when caught in the light. Amongst these objects were also a variety of other items, miniatures and jewels. I could not quite comprehend the notion that a man of no conceivable worth could possibly inherit such magnificence. It appeared that he was taken, not by the splendour of the craftsmanship, but by the wealth of compliments from those similarly naïve, who commented purely on behalf of decorum and assumption.

Thankfully the hour was growing late, and I did not have to waste my time with anymore banal socialising when we returned to the main hall, and swiftly began making my apologies. Henri's face was a mixture of disappointment and intrigue as he closed the door of my carriage, but showed no signs of suspicion.

I allowed myself a few days' reflection upon the matter, but had still to ascertain whether Henri was a worthy enough candidate for my next exploitation. Though his case was by no means a rarity, I could not waste my time upon every undeserving and contemptible man with whom I had the misfortune to cross paths. That is, until I began to hear some rather disturbing rumours.

Under the guise of hospitality and generosity, Henri had insisted his aunt take up residence on the estate, in the hope that the peaceful and comfortable conditions would aid in the recovery of her health. I soon came to learn, however, that she was being held against her will: as Henri threatened to reveal a most scandalous secret of her late husband, for whom he still harboured a fearsome hatred. Having already seen her lucrative estate pass onto his despised cousin, he was determined not to allow such a rare collection escape his evil grasp.

Disgusted though I was with such a notion, I contacted

Henri, and allowed myself to be courted for several weeks. I insisted that he should write to me under the pretence of decorum, but in reality so I could learn to duplicate his script. Being a hapless fool, he remained oblivious as arrangements were being made in his name for the shipment and sale of his most beloved collection. It is regrettable that I will not be present to witness his dim expression as the authorities, already in possession of the stolen items, hand over a perfect replication of his script upon a ticket addressed to London for later that week.

In matters of delicacy, it is often advisable to function alone, for it is a great detriment when reliance is placed upon another, particularly in cases of the utmost subtlety. But, despite my trepidation, I would require a confederate to drive my carriage to the estate and rendezvous with me at an exact time and location. Fortunately, I had become acquainted with a suitable accomplice during my time spent in Montpellier. Franck was not a gentleman by any means, and would have been completely out of his depth in a discussion upon more cultural topics; but never had I seen a man more accomplished behind the reigns. Though I was not anticipating the need for such skill, it is always safer to cater for such eventualities, and had therefore arranged to meet him in a rather distasteful drinking establishment the following evening.

My profession often takes me to places of ill repute, but the threshold I found myself upon was of such notable depravity that it had to be ranked with some of the worst in Europe. The heavy wooden door reluctantly swung on its hinges to unveil a repugnant smell that instantly stained the nostrils.

I stepped inside; the light offered no inkling as to the cause of such unpleasantness, and my eyes struggled to adjust to the thick swirling haze of smoke and despair. It was a dark, dank, squalid environment, one where only the lowliest creatures descend upon having been spat out from the very dregs of society. The civilised ignore the existence of such dwellings; but if you are in the business of exploiting their misfortune, you will find no place more suitable.

I went to purchase a glass of beer from the bar, and was served by a giant bear of a man in a tattered white apron. His enormous arms were thatched with thick dark hair, and his ruddy face bore all the signs of copious alcohol consumption. I accepted my drink, but found its resemblance to ale was not in taste, but in its effect upon the mind.

Rather than keeping company with the collection of tortured souls found filling the majority of the room, I opted for a more private booth upon the periphery. But, as I awaited the arrival of my confederate, I experienced a strange occurrence, an inexplicable sensation which I could not explain.

There was a man sitting at the bar who I had seen upon arrival: he had wild, unkempt hair covering both his head and face; his clothes could have once been described as fashionable, had they not been tattered and frayed beyond comprehension. Though his attire was regular for such an establishment, the way in which this man smoked was most peculiar. He had a faraway gaze, as if he was not really present at all. The room was filled with vacant expressions; but this did not appear to be the regular glaze caused by substance.

I remained momentarily paralysed as a sense of bewilderment transformed my expression into one of dull duplication. Never in all my exploits can I recall such a distraction. The man captivated me.

To my embarrassment, I was in such a trance that I

had not even registered the arrival of my associate, who was now holding out his hand, a questioning look across his brow. I half-rose from my seat and accepted the offered greeting, apologising for my apparent snub. He began to talk, but I confess that my attention had drifted back over to the bar, where the mysterious stranger had since disappeared.

Unnerved that I was becoming as mundane as the company I had been keeping, I decided that Montpellier was no longer a desirable place to reside. I therefore concluded my business and descended back into the cover of darkness to my nearby lodgings.

I was sure that I had not been recognised by the mystifying smoker, but I was unnerved by the possibility of having been too carefree with my appearance, and so avoided that particular establishment for several days. I spent the remaining time in a state of tedium, ensuring that I had not neglected any minor detail in my design. Franck would meet me outside my lodgings at seven, drive me to the de Saint-Hippolyte estate, and await my return. He would then take me to the port, where I would sail immediately for Palermo, and then to Athens. Such diligence is absolutely crucial to a successful operation: like an artist sketching a masterpiece, it is the often unappreciated craft of my profession.

I left my lodgings on Friday evening with both relief and adrenaline coursing through my veins, the deep blood-red of the sun sank into the horizon, a great stream of crimson oozing across the sky. My associate awaited me upon the corner, his ever-growing shadow enticing me toward the carriage. I stepped in, thanking him for his generosity, when suddenly the door slammed shut with a definitive clunk. I began to bang furiously upon the window, when a haunting bodiless voice addressed me from outside the carriage.

'I would not draw attention to yourself, Miss Adler, or you shall find yourself in considerable danger. I suggest you remain silent until we reach our destination, where I again urge discretion; you shall discover all the answers to your questions there. But for now, I shall merely say that it would not have required setting fire to Monsieur de Saint-Hippolyte's house, as I did to your lodgings so many years ago, to discover the location of your evening's endeavours.'

Such was the state of my agitation that I almost entirely ignored my abductor's final remark, the repercussions of which caused me to almost faint with shock. The absurdity was almost too much to comprehend; having spent so many years longing for such a terrible truth to be false, here I was almost three years after his death, being kidnapped by Sherlock Holmes.

I remained in a condition of nervous exhilaration until we finally reached our destination.

'We must get you inside straightaway, Miss Adler,' said the voice. 'Do not hesitate; it is now most dangerous for you to be recognised in public.'

Following Holmes's orders, as soon as my carriage was unbolted I followed him swiftly into a small rustic dwelling, doing my utmost to conceal my features. Holmes slammed the door and swooped around the room, plummeting us into near total darkness. I heard the soft scrape of a match as the dishevelled qualities of his disguise flickered into view.

'I must leave you, Miss Adler. Disguise yourself using whatever attire you deem most fitting, and for the life of you, do not answer this door to anyone other than myself.'

Without so much as a smile or hint of recognisable pleasure, Sherlock Holmes disappeared back into the night, as if he had materialised out of those dreadful mists of Reichenbach for only a second to save me from what appeared to have been imminent disaster.

I awaited his return. The room was rather small, with a fireplace suitable for only a few logs, situated between two doors, which led to separate bedrooms. Before the fire were two unstable looking chairs, and a misshapen table, upon which was a great mass of press cuttings from across Europe, but mainly those which focused upon England or France. With little else to occupy my time, I took a seat by the unlit fire and began to muse as to how the evening's events could have possibly taken such a bizarre turn. It appeared however, that I had been clearly affected by the excitement of recent events, for the sharpness of my thoughts merely reflected the feeble glow of my candle. I continued in this daze for some time, my eyes transfixed upon the slow descent of wax as it slipped silently toward the holder. Mercifully, I was eventually rescued from my limbo by the unmistakable grind of lock and key.

'I must congratulate you, Mr. Holmes,' I said, approaching him as he entered the room, stopping only inches before him. 'I have never suffered the embarrassment of being caught off guard, even by you. Still, you have had many years practice since our last encounter, and I was at the distinct disadvantage in believing you to be dead, which is hardly fair. I assume you were to take me to the authorities? It was awfully kind of you to bring me here instead.'

'I have been engaged on several cases,' said he, walking into the centre of the room in a rather unconvincing attempt to hide his discomfort. 'So I admit to not giving yours my full attention. However, after I heard some rather curious murmurings, I investigated and discovered your designs for Monsieur de Saint-Hippolyte's inheritance, and acted accordingly. My original plan was to simply lock you in your carriage and drive you to the estate; where, as you correctly deduced, the authorities were waiting for you. It was not until I laid eyes upon you this very evening that I realised just whom I had been dealing with, and forcing me into rather abrupt evasive action.'

'As brilliant in death as you were in life, Mr. Holmes,' I said, walking past and taking a seat.

'Quite,' said he, perching upon the chair opposite. 'But, so we do not have to retrace this ground later on, I *am* dead. That is something which I wish you to bear in mind; it is of the utmost importance that this belief continues. So much as a whisper of my present earthly status would put you and me in considerable danger.'

'Of course, Mr. Holmes. But may I ask, how is it that you are still alive? I read Dr. Watson's touching account, and I, along with the rest of the world, believed you to be dead. It was so heartfelt that I could not believe it to be a falsehood.'

'You are too kind, Miss Adler; but I am afraid to say dear Watson does truly believe that I have gone; that is the simple truth behind his, as you put it, rather touching account. I wish I could communicate with him, but it would place us both in a most unnecessary jeopardy' he remarked, taking the long poker from the fireplace and shifting the cold ash, as if it had some form of meditative affect upon his mind.

'As for my survival, I recall that Watson described how the contest between Professor Moriarty and myself could end in only one way; clearly, as you have surely deduced, that is not true. The Professor was kind enough to allow me to write to Watson; but as soon as I had finished, he sprang a most murderous attack upon me. It was through my knowledge of baritsu, a Japanese form of wrestling, that I was able to gain an advantage over the Professor. It was a great struggle, Miss Adler, and there were several instances where Watson's account could have become reality. But, in the end, it was I who remained on that perilous ledge, standing exhaustedly, listening to the sound of Moriarty's terrible last cry, as it crashed and reverberated down that merciless shaft. I often wonder whether even those purest of waters would be sufficient to cleanse itself of the evil which now poisons its current.'

'But Dr. Watson commented that there were no returning footprints. In that terrain, it would have been impossible to have left undetected,' said I, consumed by his narrative.

'Watson's account was inaccurate in regard to only one description. He claimed that the cliff face was insurmountable; that was not so. I realised the advantageous position I was in; if I could simply climb to safety and allow events to unfold, then I would be free to pursue my career with all my foes believing that I had perished along with Professor Moriarty. Alas, this was not to be the case. I saw Watson return to the scene of my supposed demise. I restrained myself from calling out to him, but once he was out of sight, I was attacked by Colonel Sebastian Moran. It was fortunate that it was almost completely dark, for against the cliff-face I was a difficult target. A barrage of bullets rained down around me, and I felt the deathly caress of metal shaving my flesh. Once the Colonel had exhausted his ammunition, he adapted his strategy to the rather cruder method of hurling large rocks. I had no choice but to descend back down onto the path from which I came. It was a perilous climb, Miss Adler; you can scarcely imagine the danger of the descent. On more than one occasion I believed I would be joining the late Professor; but when I did finally have the misfortune to fall, battered and bloody though I was, it was onto the path. I took flight into the night; not even Moran could be certain of my fate.'

'But why remain hidden for so long if this Moran suspects you to be alive?' I asked.

'Colonel Moran is now the leader of Moriarty's former, and distinctly reduced criminal empire, but he is still capable of inflicting damage upon a rather large scale. I remain hidden to avoid the unwanted attention of the man, but also in the hope that one day he will allow himself to be lulled into a false sense of security. Then, and only then, will I make my return.'

'That is a truly remarkable account, Mr. Holmes, but why are you in Montpellier of all places? It is far too mundane for the foremost champion of the law.'

'I have travelled under many identities, as you can see,' said Holmes, casually waving his hand across his person. 'I conducted some of my old activities in Norway, whose criminal has still at least some imagination, and provided me with a few cases of interest. I have also visited Tibet, Persia and Mecca. There is much to be said for visiting such places, but I confess, I am scarcely possessed with any great desire to return to but a single one. I was conducting some research into coal-tar derivatives in a laboratory the other side of Montpellier, but discovered all I wished to know and have since taken residence in this establishment. It offers simple comforts and the privacy which I desire; I try not to conduct many investigations, for I do not wish to attract any unwanted attention.'

'Yet you became involved in my affairs. May I ask why you wished to aid that most deplorable of creatures?'

'Having taken an interest in your case, I began to observe your movements. It struck me as rather odd that letters from Monsieur de Saint-Hippolyte were being delivered to someone who I had previously believed to be a man. I therefore followed you upon your next outing, and discovered your design to sell the offending gentleman's rather prized collection of valuables to one Charles Augustus Milverton. I concluded that you had duplicated the script of your admirer and were simply going to rob him of his inheritance. Had you opted for a different buyer, Miss Adler, I may not have involved myself with the case at all, but I could not allow the collection to be sold to such a fiend. He is the most despicable man in London. But now that I have heard of your disdain, I cannot help but wonder whether your motives were a little more unselfish, and infinitely more devious.'

I had no desire to provide Holmes with the praise he was searching for, and so merely smiled noncommittally at his theory and rose from my chair.

Over the next few months, I became rather well acquainted with Sherlock Holmes. Though we had to maintain our disguises in public, we removed our facial disguises when in the safety of his lodgings. It is a cruel twist of fate to be consistently flattered by the mundane, yet ignored by the extraordinary. Ever since our first brief encounter, I had been captivated by the great detective: yet only through my tales of triumph and frustration over Europe's many authorities was I successful in eliciting from him a response of genuine merriment.

'Oh, how superb your talents are, Miss Adler,' he remarked as he paced up and down the small room. 'You have an extraordinary gift for crime; not only do you succeed, but you leave the authorities infuriated and utterly perplexed. I have been telling Watson for years that the official force has many qualities, but their insistence upon routine, accompanied by their distinct lack of imagination, will be their downfall. How wonderfully you have proven my theory!'

'I thank you, Mr. Holmes,' I replied. 'But I cannot help but ask; why is it that you spend your time with Dr. Watson? He appears to me to be quite un-extraordinary.'

I instantly regretted my remark for the first genuine flicker of irritation shot across Holmes's expression, and he abruptly ceased pacing.

'My friend is, despite your misguided impressions, Miss Adler, a distinctly remarkable fellow,' said he, staring, as he so often did, into the distance. 'I assume your conclusions come from his publications? But I can assure you that despite my numerous requests upon the matter, he modestly depicts himself in such a way for dramatic purposes; he seems to think the public respond more favourably to such a technique.'

'I apologise, I should have realised that you would not befriend such a man if he was completely devoid of interest.'

'No need for apologies, Miss Adler,' said he, returning from his trance to face me. 'Watson himself is often guilty of remarks that I react, perhaps a trifle too hastily to.'

I had found myself fascinated by the tales of Sherlock Holmes; but in response to this unexpected note of kindness, I broke out into my first true smile since I had read Dr. Watson's account of Reichenbach.

'The Doctor may portray himself in a slightly modest

demeanour, but he certainly seems to enjoy painting pictures of women in his narratives.' I nervously enquired.

'I am told he possesses quite a talent for it; and I must admit, a slightly curious change does come over him during such cases, I have often found it rather irritating. His mind loses its keen edge when it is required most.'

'You would not speak highly of a woman in such a way, then, Mr. Holmes?'

'That would depend upon the woman, Miss Adler.'

'The Doctor painted a rather flattering image of myself in his story, 'A Scandal in Bohemia.' What did you make of his description?'

'Quite accurate; though if it were myself writing, I would have focused upon your much more intriguing deviance.'

I confess that my feelings for Sherlock Holmes developed after only a few days of our re-acquaintance, but despite my subtle inquiries into the matter, I was always greeted with an uninterested response. I believe he cared for me only as a companion. At first I could not help but feel slightly crestfallen, but when I considered how few *companions* he had, I was greatly uplifted. Though I harboured certain feelings, I refused to allow myself to suffer the embarrassment of mindless admiration. I have had the misfortune to encounter many such pitiful women, and the notion of joining their insufferable ranks was distasteful, not only to myself, but also clearly to Holmes.

I had sensed in recent days that his patience was beginning to wear thin, and though we had grown close, I was becoming increasingly apprehensive. The thick layer of smoke that now filled the lodgings surely reflected the storm clouds brewing in his mind: for such a man to remain idle for so long was dangerous. I therefore decided to engage him with what he would consider a captivating issue, for it was one of profound notoriety.

'Sherlock,' I said, as he sat in his customary silence, eyes closed and fingers drawn beneath his chin, by the cold ashes of the fire. 'You talk of Dr. Watson as a chivalrous man who would be disturbed by any crime against a woman. But one cannot help notice a rather prominent omission in his publications regarding those most terrible of crimes only a few years past.'

'You are referring to Jack the Ripper? That is a most delicate situation, Miss Adler, which it would be imprudent to comment upon publicly.'

'But we are not in public,' I pressed. 'Can't you divulge your tale to me? My imitations of Dr. Watson's chronicles are, of course, for no one's eyes but my own.'

'I see no harm; the matter has run its course and one day the truth will be published. The only logical conclusion that one can reach when presented with the facts is that Jack the Ripper was none other than Professor James Moriarty.'

'I do not doubt your answer, for I have suffered the misfortune of crossing paths with Professor Moriarty. Not in person, of course; his game was to always remain in the shadows, allowing others to dirty their hands. But pray, can't you explain how you can be certain as to your conclusions, and why must they remain unknown?'

'Not all truths are suitable in a court of law, Miss Adler. You speak of Moriarty as belonging to the shadow: that is not quite an apt description. Spiders dwell in the dark, await their prey, they adapt to their environment. Moriarty crafted his own environment, he created the shadows and dictated the movement of those inside. Does such an explanation suffice?'

'Only slightly. Surely even Moriarty did not control *all* crime. Could there not have been one knife-wielding savage who escaped his grasp?'

'Quite, but you miss the point. The Ripper was never caught: we therefore must assume that he is blessed with considerable intellect. But, if we follow my hypothesis, then the outcome dictates that Jack the Ripper was able to avoid capture, precisely because he controlled almost the entire criminal underworld. Picture Moriarty as a spider at the centre of a great web, controlling hundreds of threads; a vibration on but a single strand would be felt in the nucleus. But if the vibration is determined by the spider, not the prey, then the spider knows exactly which of its threads are quiet.'

'You mean Moriarty created crime elsewhere in order to carry out these atrocities?'

'Precisely,' said Sherlock Holmes. 'The spider creates a distraction, attacks its prey and then scuttles back into the shadow. Moriarty would have ensured that the main focus of the authorities was elsewhere by orchestrating decoy crimes, so that he could carry out the atrocities of Jack the Ripper. They were sufficient to draw the attention of the police, but never so formulaic that they aroused suspicion of any ulterior motive. The usual system of agents and buffers would have been in place; and it is fairly safe to assume that different agents were employed each time. Moriarty avoided any patterns, fooling the authorities, as well as to ensure that this most delicate of secrets was kept safe, even from his most loyal supporters.'

'Forgive me Sherlock but your reasoning appears to be rather flimsy. I do not doubt Moriarty controlled the majority of crime in London, but that by no means conclusively proves he was Jack the Ripper.'

'It does not, however I must point out Miss Adler that

were it possible to prove such, we would not be having this discussion about possibilities, for the case would be closed. As it is, the case is open, and therefore we must remain in the realm of hypothesis. Do you remember the three rather disturbing murders which took place shortly before my death?'

'Of course.'

'They were orchestrated by Professor Moriarty, and were entirely motivated by his hatred for me, and desire to halt my pursuit of him. They were meticulously executed, fiendishly violent, and yet to the public, entirely unmotivated. Do such motivations resemble anyone familiar?'

'I can understand why Moriarty would wish to murder such well-renowned figures, Sherlock, but why would he bother committing such crimes against common prostitutes?'

'The majority of our population is made up of honest men and women, Miss Adler. Murder a politician or a social reformer, and there is great scandal, but why should a man who can barely afford to feed his family and cannot vote for such people care? Brutally slaughter a helpless woman, for seemingly no reason, and everyone feels threatened. Through different methods, Moriarty terrorised all the population.'

'Your logic is as concise as always, but I still do not understand *why* Moriarty would openly risk revealing himself by killing those women. It is so out of keeping with his other exploits that it makes me question the notion altogether.'

'I need say no more than ask you to repeat your last sentence.'

'It is so out of keeping with his other exploits that it makes me question the notion altogether. You use the anomaly of his actions as a basis of his guilt?'

'You are not the first person to share such sceptical sentiments, nor will you be the last; that was the beauty of Moriarty's game. His station in society as a renowned mathematician and foremost intellect was a calculated cocoon of infallibility. Such is the foolish attitude toward social order in our country that the officials would not even entertain Moriarty as a criminal, let alone being both the Napoleon of crime and Jack the Ripper. I can only point to the circumstantial evidence, that as I closed in upon Jack the Ripper, his activities ceased. The further one advances, the further the other retreats. This was the time I began to slowly advance upon the late Professor, and he knew his game of openly taunting me was up.'

'But you could not prove it was he?'

'No, I could not. Perhaps I could, had it been my true purpose.'

'I do not understand. Capturing Jack the Ripper was not your purpose? What were you doing?'

'My purpose was to stop Moriarty, Miss Adler, not capture Jack the Ripper,' said Holmes. 'The Ripper was only one, although fairly substantial crime. I strove to bring Moriarty's criminal empire in its entirety crashing down upon him. You must understand that it was a great game being played between the Professor and me. Jack the Ripper was a classic case of diversion, and my role was to play along. I allowed Moriarty to make his move, and would then follow with the appropriate amount of intensity, whilst my attention was actually focused elsewhere.'

'You mean to say that not only did you not try to capture the monster, but you were not even trying to prevent the murders?' I exclaimed.

'I was not engaged upon the case from the start, an error in judgment that I cannot be held accountable for. But no, I did not try to prevent them.'

'But Sherlock, that is despicable!' I cried, scarcely believing this cruellest of revelations.

'Despicable? Try to recall my portrayal of Moriarty, Miss Adler; he was impregnable! Any sniff of me close to a single thread, and poof! The resolute strand of the vast web threatening to suffocate all of London would vanish, leaving me stumbling, blindfolded in the dark.'

'You mean to say even the great Sherlock Holmes was consistently thwarted by Professor Moriarty?'

'I cannot win every battle, Miss Adler, and I will not deny that Moriarty was the closest thing that I have ever had to an equal. As for the Ripper, he was the Professor's greatest achievement and his greatest mistake. The shocking nature of the crimes and the ease of his escape were designed to poison the London air with a terrible, all-consuming fear. It was also a message to myself. However, for all the Professor's cunning, his deviance and his organisation, he harboured the same flaw of all dictators; he was arrogant. The ruse of the Ripper was an obsession, and I am sure Moriarty took great amusement in consistently thwarting me in the public eye. But at last, he had provided me with an opportunity to grasp one of his great threads. Before he realised his mistake, I was striving from within, relentlessly working toward his demise. And though people may not approve of my methods, I succeeded in ridding London of both Jack the Ripper and eventually Professor Moriarty.'

'But why was this not in Dr. Watson's account? His publications have never so much as mentioned Jack the Ripper.'

'There are numerous unpublished cases of my works. It is impossible to publish such an account at this point in time. To proclaim such statements about one of our most respected scholars and citizens, with no conclusive evidence, would be distinctly unwise.'

I cannot deny that despite my initial disdain for Sherlock Holmes's ruthless nature during that fateful period in 1888, I could not help but feel an admiration toward his purely logical reasoning. Without doubt, he had defeated two of the greatest criminals the world has ever known. Remnants still remained: Moriarty's empire was in decay but still yet to collapse, while Jack the Ripper remained a symbol to all those who strove to terrorise the citizens of England's great capital. It was therefore with a heavy heart that one morning I brought news of such shocking profanity, I knew it must mean the departure of Sherlock Holmes back into the mortal world.

As I entered Sherlock's room, he was relentlessly pacing up and down, smoking his pipe at a frantic rate. The room was covered in the scattering of English newspapers, all cast upon the floor in frustration.

'He must make a move soon! I am not sure how much longer I can remain idle,' he cried.

'To whom do you refer, Sherlock?' I enquired, rather warily.

'Moran, Miss Adler, Moran! I have heard so little of his exploits that I am beginning to think that he has simply retired!'

I briefly allowed Holmes to continue in his habitual nature of muttering to himself, his manner suggestive that he was either unaware or totally unfazed by my attempted communication.

'Sherlock,' I said, surprised at the forcefulness of my tone.

'What is it?' he retorted.

'I think you may find it easier to locate the Colonel in this morning's newspaper,' I said somewhat tartly.

The unusual tone of my remark was at least sufficient to interrupt his train of thought, as he reluctantly slumped into a chair to examine the paper. One of the main articles told of a great panic which had arisen in London. It originated from a letter sent to the Central News Ltd; it read as follows:

'Holmes is gone in a watery grave
For the rest of time, no more can he save.
They thought me Moriarty, a raging Professor,
I'll prove them all wrong, when I *undress* her.
I'll do it again, stifle their cries,
Back from hell…

*Jack the Ripper will rise.'*

For a long period of time, Sherlock sat transfixed. His eyes did not so much as blink as he continued to smoke his pipe and stare at the article, as if he were willing the identity of the author to leap suddenly from the pages. It is the only instance, in my limited experience, that I can recall having seen him wear such an expression.

'Intriguing,' he finally muttered.

'I thought you said Professor Moriarty and Jack the Ripper were one and the same?' I enquired cautiously.

'They could still be so. I would have assumed it to be yet another imitator trying to strike terror into the citizens of London, but his mention of Moriarty suggests otherwise.'

'It could be Moran setting a trap?' I offered.

'That is a most distinct possibility,' he replied. 'London was, of course, the playground of Jack the Ripper, but the publication does suggest that he is unaware of my whereabouts, or indeed if I am truly alive. Nonetheless, my hand has been forced, and the only way to deduce any form of satisfactory conclusion is my slightly premature, yet long overdue return to London. Moran will not know of my disguise, and fortunately there are many different entrances to our great island.'

It would be some time before I could return to England, and I was reluctant to lose the company of Holmes. Though our time together had occasionally been fraught, he was still the most captivating man I have known.

'I will visit my brother, Mycroft, to see if he can shed any light upon this most peculiar of events,' said he, briskly gathering any item of significance. 'Should you ever require my services, Mycroft has been kind enough to maintain my rooms at Baker Street. I would urge caution and send some kind of message first; they will undoubtedly be watched, and I do not know how long it will be before I can reclaim them safely as my own. But rest assured, I will be in touch.'

# 3

# AN INTERVIEW AND A LETTER

IRENE ADLER HAD proven to be an intriguing companion during my last few months in exile. My initial impression formed from our previous encounter was quite accurate; she commanded a manipulative deviance that few possess, and it had been no exaggeration on my behalf to label her as *the* woman. However, though she may have considered our relationship to have progressed to that of friendship, I am not foolish enough to leave such a document in the hands of one of Europe's most capable criminals; and so upon my leave I commandeered her manuscript.

I journeyed back to England surrounded by the truly awful odour of what one assumed to be cargo destined for Billingsgate fish market. Moran could not search every vessel entering British waters, so I remained confident as to the safety of my passage. As the boat chugged toward London, my eyes were greeted by the charm of dense smoke and the allure of the burning furnaces below. If Watson were the one writing, I am sure he would have described the view as menacing; but having suffered the tedious tranquillity of Europe's countryside for so long, I was rather taken by the charms of industrial life.

Naturally my attention had been focused on the rather curious correspondence from Jack the Ripper. It seemed somewhat imprecise, similar in its design to the clumsy nature of a large net, rather than the delicate precision of rod and line. I was certain that, though the ensuing mass panic was intended, I was the true recipient. As to the motive behind such a ploy, I cannot be sure; if it were Moran, I can see no decipherable reason as to why he should choose that moment in time to act. The meticulous temperament of his military background would surely have demanded earlier action, particularly in light of his recently inactive status.

I remained in full disguise as I departed the boat. Though Moran could never truly be certain as to my return, I was not foolish enough to rely on any complacency on his behalf; it would have been a most unnecessary and potentially fatal risk.

It was a bitter spring evening, and a thick layer of fog had descended upon London. The street lamps were mere specks of light, which offered little consolation to those troubled by such depths of darkness. Fortunately Mycroft is a creature of frightful routine, and I was assured that it was most likely I would receive his counsel. His lodgings at Pall Mall, the Diogenes Club opposite and Whitehall, just around the corner, are his only usual ventures: only upon matters of national importance have I known him to deviate from these well-oiled tracks.

Initially the deceptive blanket of fog was a welcome aid in my safe navigation of London's streets; but once I approached Pall Mall, it caused the unfortunate necessity of approaching my brother's window, so as to ensure his predicted behaviour of reading by the fire, rather than tending to some unexpected Imperial issue.

I knocked on the door and swiftly barged past the flustered servant Geoffrey.

'What is the meaning of this?' he exclaimed. 'We do not entertain beggars. Nor do we pander to the whims of vile miscreants. Honestly, I know the French are uncivilised but to ignore the courtesy of invitation!'

'I believe my time is far more valuable than yours, Geoffrey,' said I, removing my facial disguise. 'And I assure you that I had ample reason to presume invitation.'

'Mr. Holmes!' he cried, straightening his impeccable attire. 'I apologise, sir, your appearance was so convincing that I did not recognise you for an instant.'

'No need for apologies, Geoffrey; after all, that is the function of a disguise.'

I left Geoffrey to recover from his minor ordeal and entered Mycroft's sitting-room to find him immersed in the documents of Governmental issues. It is a rare occasion indeed that such papers are cast aside, merely to allow for the tedium of guests. Though Mycroft is exceedingly capable of solving his colleague's many problems, often it is only at the request of the Prime Minister that he will eventually submit. He has a clarity of mind and a prowess for organisation which is second to none, and it is for this reason that he has formed the rather unique position as the central exchange to all Government departments. There are many within the upper-echelons of the British Government who consider him as essential; there are some who consider him to *be* the British Government, and I am told there are countless instances of his advice defining state policy.

'Mycroft, how wonderful to see you after so many years,' I proclaimed, stepping into the room.

'Dear brother, I return your sentiment, and say it is indeed a pleasure to see you looking so *alive,*' replied Mycroft, his fleshy hand grasping my own firmly. It is fortunate that the sharpness of the mind is not affected by the plumpness of one's body, for Mycroft still bore all the signs of physical idleness. His misty, watery grey eyes were surrounded by his rather corpulent facial features, while his torso disguised the feats of elegance he has been known to demonstrate.

'I thank you, Mycroft; although if my situation is as dire as this beyond the grave, I must have done something truly contemptible in my time amongst the living.'

'Yes, I heard as much from Geoffrey upon your entry; his manner is exemplary around the distinguished, but he is rather curt when attending to the less fortunate,' said he, retaking his seat. 'Still I must applaud you for your conquering of the late Professor Moriarty. You have done your country a great service, Sherlock; one for which you should be knighted.'

'I have no interest in peerage; I do not play for reward, but for the game's sake. If I accept your offer, I would be hounded further still by every authority in the land over the simplest and blandest of cases, instead of the delightfully intricate little problems which previously Baker Street so frequently provided.'

'I did not think you would consent; but once the Prime Minister learns of your triumphant survival, he will insist upon my enquiry. Anyway, I am sure we will have plenty of time for pleasantries later; I assume of course, that you have returned due to that charming letter, which has struck terror into the hearts of our poor citizens.'

'You are correct in your assumptions, difficult as I am sure they were to deduce,' said I, taking a glass of Cognac from the tray Geoffrey had so efficiently produced. 'It was my belief that Jack the Ripper was indeed Professor Moriarty; a conclusion, I recall, that we reached together. The rather abrupt end to the Ripper's activities coincided with my pursuit upon the matter, and Moriarty's death appeared to have brought a conclusive end to the case.'

'Quite so, Sherlock, it did seem to be the only logical theory. None of the Ripper cases in your absence have been anything more than pathetic imitations. However, I must point out that although this recent letter is certainly suggestive, it does by no means truly indicate the rise of Jack the Ripper.'

'You suspect Moran?' I replied.

'It would appear to me that he has become rather desperate, and has decided to adopt a rather crude method of luring you back into the lion's den; I deduce no other realistic purpose for such a course of action. But I fear you do not seem satisfied by such a theory?'

'Moran is no fool, and the use of such tactics appears a touch too simplistic for such an experienced campaigner. And why wait until now to act?'

I perceived from the hint of bewildered exasperation upon my brother's face that he was privy to information that he had yet to divulge.

'Sherlock, I know how much this Ripper business bothered you,' said Mycroft, lighting one of his beautifully fragrant cigars. 'He was the most horrendous of all criminals; but come, you cannot tell me that you have returned to hunt down an anonymous man?'

'That is my purpose,' I said.

'Sherlock, I implore you to see sense! Moran is the man you should be after.'

'Moran is *not* Jack the Ripper,' I replied.

'For God's sake, will you no longer see reason? Colonel Sebastian Moran, the right hand man of Professor James Moriarty, the man you yourself labelled the Napoleon of crime, *he* is your man!' Mycroft exclaimed, slamming his cigar down with surprising force. 'Moran may not be Moriarty, but he is still capable of damage upon a great scale; a scale that will be significantly increased if he is able to dispose of you while you are chasing shadows around the East End, protecting prostitutes from some deranged savage with a knife!'

'The sharpness of your mind always did contrast with the occasional bluntness of your tongue Mycroft,' I replied in slight amusement at my brother's little outburst. 'But fret not; you do not have to delve into your political toolbox to reason with me. As you have correctly stated, my continued existence is dependent upon my capturing Colonel Moran; however, such an exploit does not necessitate abandoning my hunt for Jack the Ripper.'

Before Mycroft had chance to retort, he was interrupted by a knock on the door, and Geoffrey entered with a perplexed look on his brow.

'I am sorry to disturb you sir, but there is a letter addressed to you. It says that it is urgent,' he said, placing the correspondence upon the table before swiftly turning upon his heel and making his exit.

'Thank you, Geoffrey,' said Mycroft. 'I do apologise, Sherlock, but occasionally my colleagues do need advice upon matters of importance.'

My mind had rather drifted into the pleasures of my smoke and the intricacies which had begun to develop when I was abruptly interrupted by the concerned tone of my brother.

'Sherlock,' Mycroft said gravely. 'This is intended for you.'

Rather shocked, I took the offending document from my brother, struggling to deduce what could have caused his dumbstruck expression. The letter resembled an authentic dispatch of the British Government, butclearly it was not another tiresome offer from the Prime Minister; the only remarkable feature judging by the gauge and texture of the paper was that it appeared to be from the Central News Ltd printing press. It read:

'I cungratulatyu on servivin the perils of RykenbackMr. Homes but I also mus' apologis for not bein the firs' to welkomyubak...' The rest was blank, apart from two small words written using red ink in the bottom-right corner of the page, *'To Hell.'*

I confess that my actions upon finishing the letter were rather rash. I leapt from my chair, Mycroft unable to so much as twitch before I had cast from my shoulders the shelter and protection which I had so readily sought. I reached the threshold, but could see nothing through the great dark cloud which had consumed London. I frantically searched the area: there was a small stone by the door, which had not been present upon my arrival; there were also the unmistakable signs of footprints. I ran to the boundary of Mycroft's property, but could see only a handful of office-clerks, rushing through the fog back to their nearby lodgings. Then I saw a most disturbing sight.

Upon the street corner, a man stepped out of the darkness. I could not see his face, for it appeared to be covered by some kind of sheath and was dressed in shadow; only his eyes could be seen, glowing demonically in the reflection of a nearby street-lamp. He wore a long black coat and top hat.

For a moment, neither he nor I could act, other than to simply remain motionless, glaring into each other's eyes. I began to run toward the man, but he simply stepped back, instantly vanishing into the darkness. I reached the corner in a matter of seconds but he had disappeared; Jack the Ripper had slipped back into the night.

I stood for a moment, transfixed; I could not comprehend how this man could possibly have known of my return. If it were Moran, then I could not help but wonder why I was still alive. A man of such ability could have quite easily shot me, or had me run down by a carriage the instant I stepped onto the street.

Aware of my fortune, I quickly returned to the now significantly reduced safety of Mycroft's lodgings. I did not have time to listen to the moaning of my brother as he awaited my return upon his step; I needed confirmation of what I had seen only moments before.

'Geoffrey!' I cried, running into the sitting room and forcing him into a chair. 'What did you see? Tell me exactly what you saw upon opening the door!'

'Mr. Holmes, what is the meaning of this?'

'Tell me what you saw, Geoffrey!' I demanded.

'There was a knock at the door,' he said tentatively. 'I opened it, but there was no-one there; I took a quick glance but I could not see anything, such was the thickness of the fog. I noticed a small stone upon the floor, weighing down the letter, and I delivered it straightaway.'

'You did not see a man?'

'At first, sir, no but, having picked up the letter, I thought I could just make out the silhouette of a man on the foot of the path. I called out to him but he did not respond.'

'What did this man look like?' asked Mycroft.

'I do not know, sir, I only saw him from behind. He appeared to be a fairly normal-sized man, and the only feature I could make out was that he was dressed in evening attire.'

'Thank you, Geoffrey, that will be all. You may retire for the evening.'

'Well, Mycroft, an interesting development indeed,' said I, retaking my seat by the fire.

'Sherlock, please, it *must* be Moran!'

'We cannot be certain who that man was until we examine the facts. This letter, for example, is a precise duplicate of a Governmental dispatch, so as to ensure that you would read the contents upon receipt. The man is therefore exceedingly intelligent: why then, did he write the letter upon paper which, though to most not instantly recognisable, is certainly discoverable, and then purposefully confuse the spelling, having previously demonstrated competence in this area? He wishes to conceal his true identity, while perhaps pointing us toward false conclusions. If this *was* Moran, why was I not disposed of in the street? It would have been far easier and far safer to ensure my death as readily as possible.'

'Sherlock, think of what you are saying. If that man *was* Jack the Ripper, yet he was *not* Moran, or a decoy, you would be forced to conclude there has been a man in London of devilish genius that has completely escaped our attention this entire time. This man would have had to have pulled the wool over both our eyes; it is an absurd hypothesis.'

'I admit such a feat is highly improbable, but surely you would not be so arrogant as to deny the possibility.'

'For God's sake, Sherlock, don't be absurd. There is only one man capable of weaving this web, and it is Professor James Moriarty!'

'Moriarty is dead, Mycroft,' I said, gazing into the fire.

'No, Sherlock, he is not.'

Such was my shock at the notion of my brother having developed a sense of humour, I turned my attention away from the embers and scrutinised his features. 'I would be fascinated to learn of how he achieved such a feat; no mortal could have survived such a fall.'

'I do not mean he *survived*, Sherlock,' said my brother, with an irritating hint of elder sibling exasperation. 'I am trying to alert your attention to the likelihood that Moran is acting upon a design inherited from Moriarty himself.'

'You believe that Moriarty ensured I shall meet the end he desired for me, regardless of his own survival?'

'You know I am correct, Sherlock; that is why you come to me with some of your problems, is it not? Moriarty, in all his infinite deviance, is the only man capable of conjuring such chaos from beyond the grave. I do not doubt for a second that it was he who was responsible for the terrible crimes all those years ago. He knew such a horrifying public taunt would haunt you more than any other; now, he is surely doing the same, before his design reaches its truly terrible conclusion. Though the most dangerous criminal has been vanquished, the most *infamous* still roams free. Surely you can see the web he has formed around you.'

'It would seem that you are indeed upon the correct path,' I conceded. 'Perhaps you can inform me of whatever it is the Colonel has been scheming, as this is the topic which clearly you are most keen to discuss; though if Moran has indeed inherited a design crafted by the hand of Moriarty, I am sceptical as to the likelihood of any tangible evidence.'

'Well, quite,' replied he, lighting a second cigar rather than suffering the embarrassment of acknowledging the minor blemish in temperament which had caused unsalvageable damage to the first. 'As I believe you once so eloquently told Dr. Watson, I am effectively the broom-cupboard of Government: I know who should be privy to certain information, but more importantly I know who should not. You may believe I am a paranoid, but you at least should appreciate the cunningness of the men we are up against, so I hope you trust my judgment when I tell you that minor snippets of inconsequential information are leaking out of Departments.'

'Minor details are often the most important, dear brother. Have you not approached any of these suspicious individuals?'

'They merely state they have heard such things in passing, or at a function where someone has had one too many sherries. Though I know them to be lying, Sherlock, it is a regrettably adequate excuse, and I can hardly interrogate them further upon such matters without sufficient cause. I am not at liberty to harass Ministers or Government employees; nor do I wish to place our adversaries upon their guard unnecessarily.'

'You intrigue me, but I fail to see any connection between your faulty Governmental plumbing and Colonel Moran.'

'Until recently, nor could I; that is, until I discovered the existence of a rather disturbing card-club. Every week, a group of gentlemen play at the Baldwin and the Cavendish. The regular attendants are the Honourable Ronald Adair of the Foreign Office; Sir John Hardy of the War Office; and a Mr. Benjamin Murray, assistant to the formidable and rather dangerous lieutenant-general of the Intelligence Division, Henry Brackenbury. At these two venues only, this trio are joined by Lord Balmoral, owner of the Central News Ltd, and Godfrey Milner, an insignificant Conservative backbencher. Now this appears to be all rather innocent, but for one peculiarity; the latter two gentlemen, for no decipherable reason, never receive invitation to play with the original trio when they intermittently visit the Bagatelle Club. One man, however, does.'

'Colonel Moran,' said I.

'Moran indeed,' he continued at length. 'I have contemplated this information for days and I can come up with no theory, other than the most sinister, which accounts for these regular players to be excluded. From what I hear, there has been no quarrel, and indeed it seems likely that neither gentleman has even been acquainted with Moran. This singularity, accompanied with the Governmental leaks and Moran's connections to some of our innermost Offices has me quite at my wit's end. I can scarcely imagine the terrible scheme that awaits this country if he is desperate enough to use Jack the Ripper simply to ensure whether or not you are in fact dead! I am in great unease; you must help me break this chain!'

'This certainly is a most disturbing turn of events, and I shall be more than cheerful to accept your offer, dear brother. Have you no further information regarding the meeting of this unsavoury group?'

'I am afraid not, Sherlock: while the attendance at the Baldwin and Cavendish are frequent and regular, the Bagatelle is sporadic. You must use your own methods to discover the date of the next meeting and, indeed, what it is that they are planning. If you are successful in breaking up this sinister band, then we may hope it will bring about not only the end of Moran and the remnants of Moriarty's criminal empire, but also prevent the rise of Jack the Ripper.'

# 4

# THE BAGATELLE-QUARTET

I REMAINED HIDDEN in the depths of the underworld for several weeks. Though I appreciated Mycroft's sense of urgency, he is often guilty of impatience: such is the way of those with no experience in the art of detection, they naively assume cases can be formulated and matters solved in a mere flash.

I decided the best course of action was to infiltrate Moran's empire via its foundations. It is often possible to gain the confidence of one of the rather mindless employees and begin to formulate a wider picture from the pieces collected from their unsuspecting tongues; if this can be achieved, such a task can be of relative ease. I used an array of dark curled hair and flat-cap to adequately cover my now unshaven face, and a tattered and frayed travellers coat sufficiently completed my ensemble of the common ruffian. I took part in several burglaries and other unsavoury dealings, but I could acquire no worthwhile information; Moran was doing his utmost to conceal his preparations. I did not have the luxury of time to weave an intricate web around this particular problem, and soon aborted such exploits; it is ill-advised to draw too much unnecessary attention to oneself, and it had become clear that a more direct approach would perhaps present more effective results.

Aware that I would be unable to extract information from the inner-trio of the 'Bagatelle-Quartet', I focused my attention upon those who made up the periphery, Godfrey Milner and Lord Balmoral.

Of the former, there is little to tell; indeed he may have been the only uncompromised gentleman in this affair. As for the latter, his newspaper had been the first to publish the recent public correspondence of Jack the Ripper, and the private message sent to myself had been written upon paper from the same print works. Due to my brother's position in society, and the slight piece of editorial work which I undertook, the letter provided what should prove to be sufficient leverage to encourage a man of Lord Balmoral's position to be of at least some assistance. Though I desired that proceedings should remain cordial, this was perhaps an unlikely outcome; matters regarding Jack the Ripper are often not met with particular relish. Fortunately, I had been previously engaged by Lord Balmoral regarding a case of the utmost delicacy, and should the situation necessitate such action, I would prematurely reveal my identity to ensure the success of my visit.

Relatively assured of my stratagem, I waved down a hansom and embarked upon my journey to Cadogan Place, in the character of a private investigator. It seemed to me rather appropriate that I began my hunt for the remainder of Moriarty's empire almost three years after seeing him plummet to his demise. I was however, rather relieved that I would not be competing in another mortal game of Chess, and even enjoyed the rare indulgence of sinking back into my seat, and momentarily casting aside all thoughts of the impending case.

Upon my arrival, the small, timid face of a child could be seen protruding from behind the curtain of one of the broad downstairs windows. There was soon a great commotion within the grand white house, suggesting that it was not customary to receive visitors announced at such an hour, for it was almost nine.

I paid my driver a small advance fee to ensure the acquiescence of his services for the rest of the evening, and tucked the correspondence of Jack the Ripper securely in my inner-jacket pocket before walking purposefully down the short shingle path, which divided the small yet elegant garden. I was saved the formality of knocking, for I was greeted upon the step by the doorman, a thoroughly displeased look upon his face.

'We do not accept guests at such an hour unless by invitation,' said he in a brisk, unquestionable tone.

'I trust, my kind sir, that you allow for exceptional circumstances?' I enquired in a thick Mancunian accent.

'You do not appear to be exceptional. State your business or be gone. I do not wish to waste my time upon the threshold all evening.'

'Nor sir, do I; I wish to gain an audience with your master, Lord Balmoral, in reference to the Bagatelle Card-Club.'

'Lord Balmoral is not a member of that establishment. I do not know who you are or where you acquired your information but –'

'I shall see to this gentleman, thank you, Stephens,' said Lord Balmoral, appearing behind the doorman. He was an aging yet energetic gentleman, dressed in patent leather shoes, matching black Kashmir trousers and smoking jacket, and a white silk shirt. 'Now,' said he, in a hushed yet aggressive tone, 'I do not know who you are, or your business, but I shall grant you a brief interview.

But I must warn you, you shall receive no comfort or advice in return for your mentioning such matters so freely upon my door!'

'As for who I am, Lord Balmoral, I am Richmond Shelvey, a private investigator sent on behalf of Mycroft Holmes. As for my business, perhaps we could step inside? I have no desire to inconvenience you any longer than is strictly necessary.'

At the mention of Mycroft's name, a visible change came over Lord Balmoral; it was clear that though he did not yet appreciate the nature of my visit, he showed all the signs of one expecting an uncomfortable conversation.

'Very well, follow me.'

I stepped inside, and the heavy mahogany door closed with a commanding thud, which echoed throughout the spacious hallway. Serene landscapes hung from the walls, and vases of flowers decorated small tables placed sporadically throughout. I am always on guard when greeted with such obvious displays of tranquillity; it is often the reflection of shimmering beauty which covers far deeper, murkier waters. I was shown into a private sitting room, and as promised, was offered no seat or comfort in the form of smoke or refreshment. Lord Balmoral stood authoritatively behind his desk, a most menacing look across his lined cheeks, and a glint of intimidation in his eye.

'Well, state your business, though I feel compelled to warn you that I am not to be taken lightly, and nor are the men of whom you so ill-advisedly referred.'

'I am perfectly aware of their reputation's; both official and otherwise. I have come to you, my Lord, in reference to Jack the Ripper.' It was most apparent that this was not the line of enquiry expected. His wrinkled knuckles stretched as the leather of the chair retreated under the tightening of his grasp.

'If you are referring to the letter which my newspaper published, Mr. Shelvey, it was sent to me anonymously. I am afraid I can offer you no information regarding Jack the Ripper, or indeed Mr. Holmes' late brother to whom the letter referred.'

'No? Perhaps you can be of more assistance regarding this,' said I, retrieving the letter and placing it upon the desk before the weary Lord.

'Mr. Holmes, I welcome you back... *To Hell,*' he mumbled. The colour washed from his expression, leaving only a pale shade of bleached terror. 'I assure you I have nothing to do with this!' he exclaimed.

'Your newspaper was the first to publish the latest correspondence of Jack the Ripper, and now a rather threatening message has been delivered to a top-level Government Official, upon paper used by your newspaper. I suggest, for the good of your business and indeed your professional reputation, that you divulge any information which might be of interest to Mr. Holmes.'

'I have nothing to say to you!' he cried. 'How dare you try and blackmail me in my own home! Do you have any idea of what you are getting yourself caught up in?'

'In fact, I rather think I do,' said I, dropping my accent and shedding my disguise.

I am quite certain that had my host not already had such a firm grip upon his seat, he would surely have fallen in sheer horror as he learnt the true identity of his guest.

'Now,' said I, taking the seat which had failed to be offered upon entrance, 'if you do not value your honourable reputation, perhaps you will be more forthcoming if I were to guarantee a visit to your wife and family regarding that lovely little scandal you brought before me.'

'My God,' he whispered, falling heavily into his chair. 'I do not believe my eyes!'

'Oh come Lord Balmoral, a man of your station should not be so dramatic! Are you not accustomed to receiving the same visitor upon more than one occasion? Though I must say, the evidence rather suggests this is not the case. After all, you have failed in your duties as host to offer me so much as a glass of water. Perhaps a measure of your rather fine whisky would be welcome to both of us. Don't worry, I shall attend to such trivialities.'

The wide-eyed astonishment of Lord Balmoral as he gawked at me from behind his desk was rather amusing, but upon swallowing a rather large gulp of his superbly sharp scotch, he was once again invigorated back into speech.

'I shall tell you what I know, Mr. Holmes. I do not know what Colonel Moran is planning, though I have cause to believe that it will be dangerous and upon a rather daunting scale. He is most paranoid regarding this design, and that is why I am not permitted to attend meetings at the Bagatelle Club; it is for discussions of the utmost delicacy, without attracting any unwanted attention. With regard to the letter from Jack the Ripper, it was, as you have presumably already deduced, sent to me personally, yet anonymously. I, of course, was instantly aware of its potential for selling copy; but its reference to you, Mr. Holmes, intrigued me most of all. I consulted the Colonel, and he told me to print it at once, for finally he would be able to ascertain your fate; something which, I am told, came to be quite an obsession in recent months. As to this recent correspondence that was sent to your brother, I cannot say; in fact, I would find it most surprising if any man other than the Colonel himself, or perhaps Ronald Adair, could divulge the information which you seek, for they are the ringleaders behind whatever operation is being set in motion. It is possible in this scenario that Adair is the more likely culprit; he works in the Foreign Office, and his father is Governor to one of the Australian Colonies, so certainly he would be in a position to create such a duplicate. Not only this, Mr. Holmes, but it has recently come to my attention that Moran and Adair have been heard quarrelling quite belligerently, though none are aware of the cause behind this rupture. Perhaps it was the delivery of this very letter.'

'Thank you, Lord Balmoral,' said I, rising from my chair. 'You have been most insightful. But pray, where would I find the Honourable Ronald Adair this evening?'

'Tonight there is a meeting of the Bagatelle-Quartet, just off St James's Street; he shall either be engaged there, or at his residence at 427 Park Lane.'

I set off immediately for the Bagatelle Club, and though Lord Balmoral had given every assurance he would not reveal my secret, I was comfortable knowing that he would certainly not uphold this promise; Moran would not yet be the wiser, and such a course of action was necessary in order to lure him back into the wilderness.

Upon arrival, I instructed the driver to wait on the opposite side of the road, directed away from the entrance to the Bagatelle. I had no desire to risk my position, or indeed my life, with the unnecessary ruse of attempting entry in disguise. Lord Balmoral had provided me with a description of the young aristocrat, and so I had no choice but to tediously await his departure.

I had sat in my carriage for a considerable length of time before movement finally began to formulate in the entrance; but, unexpectedly, I noted that it was only Sir John Hardy and a man, who must have been Mr. Winston

Murray, who vacated the premises, into two separate carriages. There was no sign of Ronald Adair or Colonel Moran.

Disturbed by this turn of events, I awaited five more minutes before urging my driver toward Park Lane. As we rounded the corner, I knew instantly that tragedy had struck. The Adair residence was ablaze with light; crowds had swarmed together in the streets like moths drawn to the flame.

I stepped out of my cab and approached a nearby constable.

'I am not at liberty to divulge any further information, Inspector Lestrade's orders,' said he, dutifully.

'But I am a friend of the Honourable Ronald Adair; may I not speak to Inspector Lestrade? I am perhaps the last person who saw the victim alive. My name is Wilson.'

I have to say that, although I have often been rather discourteous to Lestrade in the past, it was a familiar pleasure to be in his presence upon a case once more, if only to be amused by his somewhat odd appearance. He combined a bullish physique with rather rodent-like features, and was famed for his headstrong instinctive attitude toward detection. Though clearly he had gained little in the art of deduction, it was at least clear from the tweaking of his wire-thin moustache and control of the situation that he had lost none of his commendable vigour and zealous temperament.

'Inspector Lestrade, sir,' said my escort. 'This gentleman, Mr. Wilson, claims to have information regarding the victim.'

'Ah yes, thank you, Mayhew,' said he, then to me, 'Please follow me; we shall go somewhere slightly more private.' I followed Lestrade out of the hallway and into one of the small downstairs smoking-rooms. It was adequately furnished, though clearly not used for entertaining guests.

'You received my wire, Lestrade?' I enquired.

'Indeed I did, Mr. Holmes; a pleasure to have you back amongst us, sir,' said he, grasping my hand firmly.

'I should think so, three unsolved murders this year alone, and from my brief exposure to this residence, soon to be a fourth.'

'We can't all go on holiday for three years and return at our leisure, can we?'

'Quite, but I must say it appears that you need the practice far more than I.'

'Well, why don't you show off like you used to then? I assume you aren't here by coincidence. How about you inform me of what is going on here tonight? I tell you it's a real corker, and I, for one, am stumped.'

'You are quite right, Lestrade, I am not here by coincidence; currently I am pursuing a case on behalf of my brother, Mycroft. There are some highly suspicious activities occurring within the upper-strata of the British Government, and it appears that the Honourable Ronald Adair was rather embroiled in it. I cannot tell you the details, Lestrade, but if you provide me with the facts, I can give you the method of murder and the identity of the murderer himself.'

'Well, it's good to see you've lost none of your confidence, Mr. Holmes. See what you make of this one. The Honourable Ronald Adair returned here at ten o'clock this evening, from the Bagatelle Card Club. He entered his sitting-room, found upon the second floor; a fire had been previously lit and the window opened as it smoked. His mother and sister were out visiting a relation, and upon their return at eleven-twenty, tried to gain entrance to Adair's sittings, only to find the door locked from the inside and no answer to their calls. Alarmed by such a prospect, they called the servant, who forced the door and found the Honourable Ronald Adair lying on his back, murdered in cold blood. Those familiar with the victim once described him as youthful and moderately handsome, but you cannot see any of that anymore, Mr. Holmes. His head has been horrifically mutilated by an expanding revolver bullet. However, there was no trace of a murder weapon, nor were they any footprints or signs of disturbance in the shrubbery some twenty feet below. No one else had been in that room. The only other point of interest was that Adair had been writing a list of names with some figures next to them; in accordance with his earlier destination, I believe them to simply be a record of his winnings. Before you arrived, Mr. Holmes, I was inclined to suspect Adair had cheated someone he rather shouldn't have.'

'That is all?' I asked, unsurprised by this terrible, yet rather convenient outcome.

'Indeed, sir, it is,' replied Lestrade, slightly taken aback by my tone.

'Thank you, Lestrade, your description was most enlightening. Now, I shall be able to tell you exactly how this little conundrum unfolded and the culprit behind it; all I require in return is your total obedience upon my every instruction.'

'Ha! Oh that's all is it? Very well, Mr. Holmes, anyone else and I would have been up in arms at such a suggestion. Now, what is it that you have in mind?'

To his great credit, Lestrade agreed to remain idle despite my revelation, and dutifully allowed the murder of Ronald Adair to transform itself into what became known as 'The

Park Lane Mystery'. I was grateful that Scotland Yard still failed to employ or promote the qualities required to solve such a case: quite clearly, there was only one theory to suit the facts. Frustrating though it was to allow these events to continue, it was also of the utmost importance to put Lestrade through such an ordeal.

The first of which was simply to allow Moran to simmer in a fit of agitation. I was certain that he would have heard of my return through Lord Balmoral, and it was now necessary to play a most dangerous game of cat and mouse.

The second was one which I had eagerly anticipated. I had kept my eye upon the developments around Park Lane in the hope that its shocking crime, yet subtle points of interest, would spark the embers of curiosity in an old friend. It was with both a cause of personal pain and amusement that I listened to some of the whimsical theories being proclaimed to the hoards in the streets by plain-clothed detectives. I stood upon the Oxford Street end of Park Lane, disguised as a decrepit book-collector, and listening to yet more absurd tales from a rather lean man with sapphire-coloured glasses, when, to my delight, I noted the appearance of a rather fine-looking fellow. He was tall and well-built, with neatly trimmed hair and moustache, and his impeccable conservative attire smacked of time in the armed forces. I had avoided making contact with Watson, as I wished not only to avoid placing my dear friend in a most unnecessary peril, but also to guard from any act of momentary weakness on his behalf if he sought to contact me. Happily, however, such precautions were no longer required.

I moved to the periphery of the crowd which had gathered, and positioned myself behind Watson, noting the visible signs of his agitation at the ridiculous observations being offered. As he turned in apparent disgust to continue upon his way, I quite purposefully knocked into him, sending my selection of rare collectibles tumbling into the street.

'My dear fellow,' he said. 'I do apologise, please allow me to assist you with your books.'

Although I was confident that Watson would not recognise me beneath my self-designed hump, time-hardened features and notably reduced height, it was critical that any meeting take place under seemingly innocuous circumstances. And so I simply snarled at my friend and disappeared amongst the swarm, and maintained a safe distance as I followed him, curiously, to Baker Street.

I waited an adequate amount of time before knocking upon my door, which was swiftly answered by my dear housekeeper Mrs. Hudson. She was a rather small, middle-aged woman, who was fiercely loyal, and had shown great instinct during my residency at Baker Street. On more than one occasion she had provided invaluable assistance, to which I shall be forever indebted. For the time being, however, I decided it would be imprudent to reveal my true identity and so enquired of an oblivious Mrs. Hudson whether I would be allowed entry to thank the charitable gentleman from the street.

My rooms had been kindly maintained by my admirable housekeeper and subsidised by Mycroft. I like to believe my rooms were cheerfully yet practically furnished: as it is necessary to make one's clients feel welcomed and relaxed if they are to divulge their private affairs. The only new additions were some rather curious objects which had not been intended for my address.

'I came to apologise for my rough manner,' said I, addressing Watson in a croaking voice. 'I realise my reaction was unfitting toward such a charitable offer.'

'You make too much of such a minor token of goodwill, sir,' he said, standing in the middle of our old quarters. His hands, it appeared, reflected his state of mind, for they seemed to be hopelessly searching, buried deep down into his empty pockets.

'Perhaps so, sir, but no matter my hardships, I was raised to always show gratitude to those who deserve it. I see you are a busy man, and I will not attempt a sale upon you; but I will offer a kind word of advice. There is a gentleman with a rather formidable reputation around these parts; I do not know him by name, but I saw him follow you and stop just across the street as you entered.'

With a look of bewilderment across his features, Watson turned and slowly approached the window.

# 5

# A SYMPHONY OF GLASS

I COULD NOT fathom the identity of the daunting pursuer of whom my guest spoke: few men commanded such a reputation, and I could see no reason why I should be followed by such a man. I had visited Baker Street upon several occasions over the last three years, and I did not believe for an instant that my military background would have abandoned me so readily; I would have almost certainly become aware of such a presence during my visits. But, as I stood and contemplated my predicament, my heart was clenched by the grasp of fear.

This was the first occasion I had visited Baker Street since the predicted rise of Jack the Ripper. Holmes had never shared with me whether he had even a scrap of incriminating evidence; but if he had, surely it would be sufficient to cause Moriarty's old followers to now abandon Moran in disgust. Had the Colonel been watching the rooms? Perhaps he had been unsuccessful in a search of his own, and believed that I would take him to such information. Though the rooms showed no sign of disturbance, it was perhaps still premature to draw any firm conclusions. Aware that it would be far too easy to constrict myself into a riddle of paranoia before I had even ascertained my situation, I decided to investigate my now rather precarious position.

Holmes's old revolver was still in the desk; I knew my chances were slim against Moran, but it at least offered some protection. To the great surprise of my guest, I withdrew and loaded the weapon. His eyes glistened with the pale-white of fear as I motioned for him to be seated and remain calm. I pressed my back against the right-hand wall and edged closer to the window. The drawn out metallic click of the revolver reverberated with murderous intent.

Ensuring only the smallest fraction of my face was visible through the glass, I tentatively peered down into the street below. It was a rather busy day, and the street was a constant stream of people and carriages, but there was no man who matched the description the book-collector had offered. I remained by the window, desperately trying to devise some of form of escape, when I heard a most shocking sound.

'It is good to see you have not let your guard down after all these years, my dear Watson,' said a hauntingly familiar voice.

For a moment I remained in a state of complete paralysis. The tone was unmistakable, yet I knew the owner to have been dead for almost three years. Terrified that I had been led into a trap, I decided immediate action was crucial. I dropped to the ground, and spun around onto one knee, my fully loaded revolver now pointing directly into the temple of my guest.

'Move an inch and I shall shoot,' I warned, rising to my feet. 'You knock into me in the street, warn me of a dangerous man who is nowhere to be seen, and now try and imitate the voice of my late friend Sherlock Holmes. Explain yourself man!'

'As to your first points, Watson, they were rather for my own amusement, and as for the latter, I am rather offended that you believe me to be a mere imitation.'

'I do not have time for this nonsense,' I replied. But as I made to direct this rather disturbing individual toward the door, he began to remove his hair, from both his scalp and whiskers. To my wide-eyed astonishment, the man who stood before me had a long nose, sharp jaw, and piercing eyes. It was none other than Sherlock Holmes.

'Good God, Holmes!' I cried, almost keeling over at the shock. 'Is it really you? I can scarcely believe my eyes! You almost gave me an aneurism! For a moment I believed I had fallen prey to some deadly deception.'

'I apologise for my rather imprudent choice of revelation, but you know of my fondness for the theatrical,' said he, amused at my misfortune.

'Indeed I do, Holmes,' I replied, years of mourning mixing with almost contemptuous rage. 'If I were not so entirely thrilled by your presence, I would be sorely tempted to thrash you!'

'Ha! Good old Watson, I do apologise, and it is duly appreciated that you have refrained from thrashing me.'

I looked on in amazement, as Holmes shed the rest of his disguise. He now stood, dressed in an elegant suit, pristine in condition, other than the slight unkemptness created by the slumped position that he had forced himself to adopt. His white hair and hump were cast casually amongst the volumes he had placed upon the table. Although still rather gaunt, Holmes looked in much better health and temperament than when we last spoke, upon that fateful eve at Reichenbach. He took time to walk about the room before we shared a most rare, brotherly embrace.

'Come, Holmes,' said I, placing the revolver back into

the drawer before taking a seat; a chair I had not brought myself to use in over three years. 'How on earth did you survive that perilous fall?'

'Well, Watson,' said he, taking his place and lighting his pipe. 'In my experience, I have found a truly remarkable solution to surviving such a fall. It really is one of my more astute ideas, being both simple and effective.'

'Do tell,' I urged, but Holmes seemed more than content to gaze around under the pretence of sentiment, teasing my curiosity.

'You know I have truly missed some of the comforts of these rooms, Watson. I have lived a life of distinct discomfort these past years.'

'Holmes,' I said impatiently.

'I have found, dear Watson,' said he, turning to face me, 'that the best way to survive such a fall, is to rather simply… not to.'

'To not to? As in *not to fall*… Holmes, you are infuriating!' I exclaimed, as he allowed himself a minor chuckle at this most dramatic of anti-climaxes.

'I apologise,' said Holmes. 'Professor Moriarty was indeed generous enough to allow me to write you the note which you read, and I truly did believe my career to be at an end. It was both skill and fortune which allowed me to survive, but I was quite prepared for a more final conclusion.'

We both remained in a thoughtful silence. Though I was hurt that my closest of friends had deceived me in such a manner, and for such a prolonged duration of time, I could not help but be awed by the sacrifice he had been prepared to take.

'I am surprised you have not asked how I managed to survive Watson,' said Holmes after a prolonged period of reflection. 'Having scribed such a convincing, yet inaccurate account I thought you would wish to know the details.'

'If you are willing to talk about such events now Holmes then please by all means.'

I can scarcely recall such an ordeal, even from our adventures together. Even for an experienced campaigner, the terrible image of Holmes and Moriarty grappling and teetering upon the edge of that dreadful abyss sent the tingling sensation of horror shivering down my spine. Though I pride myself on my ability to crack on in such perilous conditions, I confess I was more than pleased not to have heard the terrible last cry of Moriarty as he plummeted into that seething cauldron.

'Your tale is a remarkable one, Holmes, but I do hope you will provide as sufficient an explanation as to why you have deceived me for so many years,' an air of bitterness still ringing in my voice.

'Watson, if I keep apologising we shall be here until dawn,' said he. 'I know your practice has been more than a trifle dull, and I truly did take to my pen when I heard of poor Mary's untimely death; but I could not risk my position.'

'No, I understand, old chap.'

'Speaking of Mary, if I may,' said Holmes, to my surprise, 'I cannot help but notice that you have used my lodgings to dispose of those rather heartfelt gifts I had purchased for you both during my exile.'

'Those were from you?'

'Certainly; this Vigor's home exercise horse for instance,' said he, pointing to a ridiculous wooden contraption. It bore more resemblance to a mechanical crate than a horse; its foolish bouncing mechanism was most uncomfortable and it would have been the height of embarrassment to be seen upon such a device.

'Holmes, unless one had suffered a rather unfortunate blow to the skull, why on earth would one wish to possess such a contraption?'

'The advertisement clearly stated that it is a complete cure for obesity, hysteria and gout. I assumed being both loving husband and a doctor, that you would have been quite cheerful at the prospect of your wife avoiding such issues. I hear even the Princess of Wales has one.'

'And that ridiculous male corset?'

'I recalled Mary's culinary talents and thought you may have gained a few pounds, which you may have wished to remain a private affair. After all, it is of the highest importance that a doctor at least appears to be healthy.'

'Holmes, what would be said of me if my former servicemen heard that I wore a corset? I would never be able to show my face at the club again.'

'You are supposed to wear it *beneath* your clothes Watson, so as to conceal the item. Surely you do not believe I purchased such gifts simply for my own amusement?'

'Oh no Holmes, I am sure the image of me bouncing up and down on a wooden box, wearing what most would consider a female undergarment would not amuse you in the slightest.'

'Well, entertainment is limited in the afterlife, Watson,' said Holmes. 'Now, to business, my good fellow; you will need to remove these items and take them back to Kensington where they belong, I have need for these rooms once more. And so, if I may be so bold, do you Watson, should you be willing to take up your former residence once more?'

'Mrs. Hudson!' I cried. 'Sorry, old boy, but if you are to go into your usual amount of detail we will need some tea.'

'Ah, Mrs. Hudson,' said Holmes, rising from his chair, 'how wonderful it is to see you again.'

'Mr. Holmes!' she exclaimed, clutching the door to prevent herself from falling. 'This is the most unexpected of pleasures! But I hope you have not returned from beyond the grave to haunt me with your eccentricities?'

'But my dear woman, why else would I be here?' replied Holmes. 'I am sure you will have ample time to complain of my habits later, but for now I am a trifle famished, and Watson is being made to await a truly fine tale. If you could bring us some tea and two plates of your fine luncheon, I would be most grateful.'

Along with the whole of the country, I had of course read the correspondence from Jack the Ripper. I consider it to be the first duty of any man to protect a woman, no matter what her circumstance. My blood had boiled, and I had had stern words with any children I passed playing in the street who were naively re-enacting his terrible legacy.

Despite my publications and association with Holmes, I have always looked on in disgust at the relish of the public for such events. The fascination of murder has an immoral place in our society, and to revel in such violence is a notion I find most repulsive. Melodramas fill theatres: street-ballads and ale-house songs amalgamate and echo throughout the city; and I even hear how murder-souvenirs are savoured by those who can afford such perverse luxuries. Though his crimes may have ceased, I found no comfort in the knowledge that the beast may simply be lying dormant, waiting in the shadows. It therefore came as a great delight that we were about to end this most infamous of chapters in London's great history.

'It must be Moran,' I remarked after Holmes had finished his narrative.

'Mycroft drew the same conclusion. He is convinced that it was a ploy of the Bagatelle-Quartet.'

'Have you any theories as to their activities?'

'Nine, but that is immaterial to our investigation at this time, for now we have more decisive work on our hands than to speculate over mere conjecture.'

'Capture Moran and await the affect; or catch Jack the Ripper in the act?'

'Bravo, Watson, I see you are still as sharp as a hunting knife. But it is Moran who we move upon tonight, and as you correctly deduce, we shall be forced to simply await the consequences; hardly a desirable solution, I concede, but for the moment the most practical. If we are successful in our exploits, we shall bring a conclusive end to this deadly collaboration. As for Jack the Ripper, if he remains a figure of the shadows, then, although we may never truly be certain, we may rest somewhat safely in the assurance that he was most likely to have already been consumed by the depths of Reichenbach.'

'When do we leave?'

'Oh, not until tonight, but I do have a slightly unusual task which needs performing before we vacate.'

'Should we not inform Mycroft of these developments? You say he is anxious to hear of your capturing Moran.'

'No, Watson, Mycroft has faith in my abilities. A man of his position has enough on his plate without needing to hear of my every movement. He will remain upon his rails and simply be delighted with our results when we produce them at one of his stations; should he wish to hear of our methods at a later date, I am sure I will either pay him a visit, or he can simply read them through my esteemed biographer.'

The task of which Holmes spoke was indeed rather odd. He had purchased a wax bust of himself from

Monsieur Oscar Meunier of Grenoble, and the majority of our afternoon was spent recalling our exploits over the last three years, while he arranged this bust in order to perfectly resemble his posture.

'Holmes, I am aware that you can be rather fond of yourself, but is this not a touch too far?' said I, observing from behind one of the day's papers.

'It serves a far greater purpose than feeding my ego or your mockery,' said he, positioning the bust by the left-hand window. 'Ah, Mrs. Hudson, impeccable timing as ever.'

'What is it now, Mr. Holmes? I have been up and down those stairs more times this afternoon than in the entire duration of your absence!'

'I do apologise. Only one more favour do I ask of you, and it is most significant.'

'Very well, Mr. Holmes, as long as it does not place me in a compromising position in the eyes of the law.'

'No, I only like to compromise Watson; particularly upon any occasion that he needs reminding of life's more exciting elements.'

'Like riding a wooden horse?' I interjected.

'Exactly. Now Mrs. Hudson, if you would be so kind; Watson and I will have departed long before, but at exactly ten this evening, I need you to return to this room and move this wax bust,' said Holmes, waving his hand in the direction of the waxwork, dressed in one of his old dressing-gowns and set upon a pedestal table, 'upon every quarter-of-the-hour. Enter the room on your knees, and move it from the front, so as to disguise your shadow.'

'I assume that this *is* of importance, Mr. Holmes? I shall not be pleased if I discover that I have merely been playing a part in one of your silly experiments.'

'Dear woman, I would not ask you of such a service unless it was of *the most* critical importance.'

It had been some time since I had left Baker Street with the thrill of adventure coursing through my veins. I shall always cherish my years of wedlock as my most content, but still I cannot deny the void that was left in my heart since the day of Holmes's supposed death.

I had kept a keen interest in criminal exploits and read every perplexing case which so readily presented itself before the public. I even assisted Lestrade on a few occasions, though often I could only raise some minor detail of significance; I was never an adequate replacement for the brilliance of Sherlock Holmes. I had left Baker Street alone and travelled back to my Kensington lodgings to await Holmes's arrival; there we would dine and continue our discourse before setting out into the night.

We departed my quarters into a hansom at exactly half-past nine; our destination, Cavendish Square. Despite the strategic advantage we seemingly enjoyed, Holmes was in a state of great apprehension. The intermittent flashes of light from passing street-lamps provided me with only flickering glimpses of my friend. He sat rigidly compressed, and only the occasional twitch in finger or brow assured me of his consciousness. I had no desire to break him from his meditative concentration, and simply sat in a fit of nervous excitement, my hand subconsciously stroking the cold barrel of my revolver.

As our carriage drew up at our destination, Holmes's entire body seemed to tighten, as if he were being suffocated by the full-body grip of a python.

Upon exiting the carriage, he gave long searching looks down the street, assuring himself at every corner that we were not being followed. I believe there are few men, if any, with a more comprehensive knowledge of London's many paths and passages than Sherlock Holmes. We travelled through a maze of dark alleyways, stables and yards at a rapid pace. We wove in and out of this urban labyrinth, through Manchester Street and Blandford Street, before our journey finally terminated at a wooden gate and the entrance to an empty house.

Fully aware that Holmes had no prior connection to this building, I deduced, the key that he had produced from his pocket had been acquired by unlawful means. He motioned me inside, my eyes struggled to adapt to the darkness as he relocked the door, plummeting us both into an impenetrable gloom. I could scarcely see Holmes, standing only a few feet away from me, for he had insisted that under no circumstances could we justify the use of even a solitary candle.

We set off into the house; the dull groaning of the floorboards echoed throughout, alerting whatever evil that occupied such a dwelling that its nest had intruders. I was amazed at Holmes's ability to navigate in such conditions, for he seemed to barely place a foot wrong as we travelled further and further into the depths of the house.

Suddenly, I felt his cold thin fingers grasp my wrist. We stood for a moment silently waiting; the darkness seemed to almost close upon us, but nothing stirred. Satisfied, Holmes led the way down a long hall toward a dull glow in the distance. We turned left into a large empty room; a thick curtain of dust lay across the windows, forever resilient against the insufficient penetration of the outside lamps, casting the corners of the room into a deep shadow.

'Now we must wait,' Holmes whispered.

It was a cold, still night and though the rain had ceased to fall the air remained damp. Men and women could be seen tightening their coats and raising their collars as they hurried back to the warmth and comfort of their homes. Amongst the general hustle and bustle of public life, Inspector Lestrade's plain-clothed men could be spotted after half-hour intervals, seeking shelter under house doorways.

'Mrs. Hudson is doing a fine job,' I commented almost inaudibly as the silhouette of the waxwork rotated perfectly and entirely naturally. The bust of my friend had been crafted perfectly; it encapsulated all of his defining features; and, had I not been stood next to him, I would have sworn before a jury that the profile was indeed that of Sherlock Holmes.

'I would not have daunted her with such a task if I did not believe her capable. The graceful touch of a woman is far more reliable and trustworthy than having one of Lestrade's blundering fools attempt at subtlety.'

Despite all of Holmes's intricate planning, it did not appear as if our evening's endeavours would bear fruit. As the minutes turned to hours, his agitation grew from impatient tapping to frantically pacing the room: never have we remained in such purgatory. I had once again taken out my pocket-watch, and I noted the hour turn midnight when Holmes suddenly stopped in his relentless march. He remained silent as a hawk before swooping upon its prey, listening. Slowly, he lowered himself to the ground, and pressed his ear upon the floor; his features were that of the utmost scrutiny. He then rose and silently glided into the shadows of the room, urging me to join him.

My senses, though keen and alert, are incomparable to Holmes. For a moment, I could hear no sound which would cause such actions, and I wondered whether my friend's wits were coming to an end, such was the prize at stake. But then, as I joined him in the shadows, I heard the disturbance. There were slow, purposeful footsteps, almost silently echoing throughout the empty house. A door faintly creaked, and the steps began to march decisively down the corridor. Holmes pressed himself in a crouched position against the wall; I followed suit, my hand tightening around the handle of my revolver. As I squinted through the darkness, the outline of a featureless spectrefilled the open doorway. I glanced at Holmes in search of some form of reassurance, but, to my distress, his eyes appeared wide and pale; his body in a state of fear. I had heard all of the stories, read all of the articles and even been an active component in the strive to bring down this hellish creature; but I must confess that fear engulfed me, my mind betrayed me, and my blood ran colder than the terrible currents of Reichenbach at the realisation of being in the same room as Jack the Ripper. Though I had witnessed the horrors that this beast had committed, to finally lay eyes upon him was almost a perverse confirmation that he was no malevolent myth. From what I could see of the phantom-like apparition, he wore a tall top hat and long leather coat; his face was masked, yet the eyes burned. He stepped into the room and there, slightly protruding from his coat, was a long slender box, the container of his demonic blades. He placed the box on the floor and began to unpack the contents, though, rather oddly, the object met the ground with a definitive metallic thud. He removed his facial-sheath but I could not see his features, for he had his back turned to us. He began to assemble the terrible contraption, which concluded with the sharp crack of a rifle snapping into place. It was not until he slightly raised the bottom panel of the window, and the light from the street illuminated his features, that we were able to identify our man. He had a high, receding hairline and a thick moustache; a gleefully murderous expression merged disturbingly into the savage features of Colonel Sebastian Moran.

Still oblivious to our presence, Moran began to mumble, as if performing some kind of ritual. Within a matter of seconds, the rifle was breached, cocked and loaded, ready to execute the murder of Sherlock Holmes. Crouching down, Moran rested the barrel upon the window ledge; he began to inhale deeply. Though the shot was a relatively simple one, such was the value of the supposed prey that he appeared to be taking extra precautions. He took aim, gently squeezing the trigger, but waited a fraction longer than I would have expected. The look of greed was quite absurd as it contorted the Colonel's face; his eyes betrayed him, as finally, he relented and pulled the trigger. Even upon that stillest of nights, to any passers-by, the gentle tinkle of broken glass would have appeared as nothing more than a trivial domestic accident. For Sherlock Holmes, it was the great crescendo in a symphony of glass.

Moran enjoyed a brief second of euphoric triumph before Holmes hurled him face-first upon the ground. The Colonel gave a great cry of bewildered outrage and was upon his feet in an instant; his great arms flung out fearsome blows as he and Holmes engaged in a tremendous tussle. Both men were clearly more than competent in close-quarter combat, and it appeared Moran had gained a momentary advantage when he grasped Holmes by the throat. I saw my opportunity in a flash, and brought the butt of my revolver crashing down upon the Colonel's skull. He dropped like a stone, and I sprang upon him in an instant, pinning him to the ground as Holmes signalled Lestrade.

'Thank you, Watson,' said Holmes, bleeding from the mouth and slightly out of breath. 'The Colonel has lost none of his combative skill, and I am sure that you prevented a rather unpleasant ordeal.'

A moment later, the bustle of heavy and hasty steps could be heard hurtling toward the room, as Lestrade emerged, tenacious as ever, with two constables on his heels.

'Good evening, Lestrade,' said Holmes. 'As promised, I deliver to you your murderer, Colonel Sebastian Moran.'

'Well, you are indeed a man of your word, Mr. Holmes,' replied Lestrade. 'Is that the weapon which you described?'

'It certainly is,' said Holmes, who was now kneeling over Moran's airgun and examining it with the utmost exactness. 'It is a rather unique weapon. It is of German origin, crafted for the late Professor Moriarty by the blind German mechanic, Von Herder. It is almost completely silent and capable of great power. It is the first time I have seen the weapon, although I have been fractions away from being one of its many victims. It is this which the Colonel used to murder the Honourable Ronald Adair in such supposedly baffling circumstances.'

'Lestrade!' snarled Moran, 'if you are going to arrest me, make it quick! I do not wish to stand here and listen to this!'

'Ah, Colonel,' said Holmes, turning toward our prisoner, 'I do not think you are at liberty to make requests; particularly as you have not only broken my window, but also ruined what was a perfectly admirable waxwork.'

'You unbearable fiend,' the Colonel muttered.

'Well, I think after all the trauma you caused me at

Reichenbach, Colonel, I should at least be able to have my fun. Somewhat ironic, is it not, that the most accomplished heavy-game shot our Eastern Empire has ever seen was hoaxed so easily into such a familiar trap.'

This was the final tether on Moran's patience. He charged at Holmes, only to find himself being dragged back, restrained by the two constables.

'Temper, Colonel, temper. I'm sure you will have bountiful opportunities to vent your physical frustrations in one of the regular yard scraps.'

'I have had enough of this man's taunts, Lestrade! If you have sufficient reason to arrest me, then do it quickly and by the book, for God's sake.'

'If you insist,' said Lestrade. 'Colonel Sebastian Moran, I place you under arrest for the murder of the Honourable Ronald Adair and the attempted murder of Sherlock Holmes. Any other matters Mr. Holmes?'

'Yes, Lestrade. I wonder, Colonel, whether you would inform us whether it was a certain letter to my brother, Mycroft, which caused the minor quarrel between yourself and the Honourable Ronald Adair?'

'I shall not satisfy your suspicions unless I am forced to do so under oath!' spat Moran.

'Very well, though I suggest that it may be worth a confession to one of my colleagues regarding your activities at the Bagatelle Club. That is, of course, to assume that you wish to avoid the gallows? Though if you are not willing to comply, I can always take time out of my now remarkably free schedule to discover the answers myself, but it really would be a most unnecessary inconvenience. As for your proceedings,' said he, turning away from the raging, distraught Colonel, 'please do not include either mine or Mycroft's name in the involvement of this case, or as a reason for arrest. We shall have to simply fashion a rather more innocent and suitable motive behind the Colonel's actions. In fact, I must congratulate you, Lestrade! You have returned to form in spectacular fashion, and I commend you. Not only do you have your man but you uncovered the motive as well! A gambling rivalry, I believe you said? I suggest you visit Baker Street and collect the soft rubber bullet which has so recently passed through my window; I think you shall find it remarkably similar to the one responsible for the death of Ronald Adair. Watson and I shall be there for the rest of the evening.'

Upon our triumphant return to Baker Street, we found Mrs. Hudson sitting at the table enjoying a cup of tea and a slice of cake; a casual visitor would have been totally unaware of her role in the capture of London's most dangerous criminal.

'You performed your role perfectly, Mrs. Hudson,' said Holmes warmly as we entered the room. 'Did you note where the bullet went?'

'Thank you, Mr. Holmes, I trust my evening's labours served both you and Dr. Watson well. I heard quite a stir from across the street, though I dare say you gentlemen know far more about it than I. As for your bullet, it passed through the head of your bust and flattened itself against the back wall. It is so delightful to have you back, Mr. Holmes. Not one person has had the decency to shoot at my walls during your absence.'

'No? I apologise, Mrs. Hudson, I thought Watson might have obliged,' Holmes replied, picking the bullet up off the carpet. 'It is a genius combination of both airgun and soft revolver bullet. Without knowledge of the former, Lestrade and his men were baffled by the evidence of the latter. Fortunate I am that Moran used such tactics, for its singularities allowed me to completely dictate and manipulate the situation to my advantage.'

'Adair's open window; the scenario was identical to the scene you just recreated!'

'Indeed, Watson. That is how he met with such an unpleasant end.'

'It is simplicity itself,' I said. 'But what about Jack the Ripper?'

'If we run with the hypothesis that Moriarty was indeed Jack the Ripper, despite Moran's rather startling resemblance in the darkness, we can conclude that he is dead. As for recent events, we know that there was some form of rupture between Moran and Adair, the nature of which we can, for the time being, only speculate. We know Moran used the letter from Jack the Ripper to lure me back into London; and there is still the likelihood that Moran himself sent it anonymously to Lord Balmoral. Not even Moran would openly associate himself with the crimes of the Ripper. Confident that I had been consumed by Reichenbach, or perhaps through matter of personal urgency, Moran went ahead and murdered Adair, taking full control of what would have become known as the Bagatelle-trio. It must have come as quite a shock to the Colonel when he learnt through Lord Balmoral, not only of my survival, but also that I was actively investigating matters so close to his heart. Immediately, he placed agents on the lookout, and I allowed one of his sentinels to spot me entering Baker Street yesterday. Moran knew not only the success of his design, but also his freedom and perhaps even his life depended entirely upon his silencing me. I was therefore confident that it would be he who would perform the deed himself.'

'I am a little embarrassed to admit, Holmes, but I was momentarily overcome with a terrible fear when it looked as if it were indeed Jack the Ripper who had joined us.'

'It was a trifle unnerving,' said Holmes, 'but, having

heard my reading of the events, have you come to any solution for the door being locked upon the inside?'

'Adair had a piece of paper with two other names written upon it, those who completed the Bagatelle-Quartet: he had also recently quarrelled with Moran. It is possible that the two were locking horns regarding the direction of operations and Adair was attempting to swing favour by means of bribery.'

'Superb, Watson! That is the conclusion I also reached. He locked the door himself, to consider this most delicate of problems in the utmost privacy.'

'Your theory seems conclusive, Holmes,' I remarked, refilling both of our glasses with some of my old gin. 'We shall have to await the trial before it is verified, of course, but the evidence of both the rifle and the bullets will surely suffice to convict Moran.'

'Indeed,' said he disinterestedly, intently gazing out of the window. 'But I fear Moran's trial is now the least of our problems. Our celebration is at a premature end, Watson.'

'Holmes?'

'It would appear that we have failed; and unless I am very much mistaken, we shall be spending the rest of the evening examining the body of a poor mutilated young woman.'

'Holmes, what an absurd statement. How can you be sure of such a development?'

'Perhaps your gin has compromised my reasoning, Watson, but unless I am on the verge of collapsing drunkenly to the floor, I believe that the rather robust gentleman escorting Lestrade is none other than Inspector Abberline.'

# 6

# AN ANOMALY IN THE WORKS

221B BAKER STREET was not a pleasurable destination for a man of Chief Inspector Abberline's reputation. Distinguished men of the law do not willingly suffer, what I am sure they consider to be, the whimsical theories of an amateur detective such as Sherlock Holmes: but such is the nature of desperate men, that pride is cast aside only at the last. For some, Holmes represents the last court of appeal; for the official-force, he is the final chance of salvation before accepting their plummet into the professional abyss. Jack the Ripper not only terrorised citizens, he laid bare the failings and ineptitude of the force's investigative techniques. Despite this, Inspector Abberline had actively worked against the inclusion of Sherlock Holmes. It was a mistake Holmes was only too pleased to bemoan; yet, such a blatantly counter-productive manoeuvre caused a deep suspicion of the Inspector to remain in the depths of my sub-conscience.

'It is the way with men such as Inspector Abberline, Watson,' Holmes had explained, 'they will run head-first into every dead-end before accepting that someone else may know how to navigate the labyrinth. Much time and energy could be saved if my *superiors* were not inhibited in such a way, but alas, eventually the spark of desperation brings enlightenment.'

It is one of the few occasions that Holmes's explanation did not satisfy my ill feeling. For a man of stout heart, the capturing of such a monster must be held as the first priority, not the identity of the supposed hero. Abberline might have been a proud man, but I could not fathom the notion that he could place his own reputation above the life of even those most helpless of women. Such a demonstration suggested a most sinister motive on behalf of the Inspector: and when one considered his access to high-grade police intelligence, accompanied with his excellent knowledge of the Whitechapel area, I could not help but be disturbed by his hypothetical position of both hunter and hunted.

Holmes, of course, remained convinced as to the guilt of Professor Moriarty, a theory which I came to accept; but with Moriarty consumed by Reichenbach, and Moran provided with an alibi, old feelings of foreboding had been resurrected along with the demonic rise of Jack the Ripper. Holmes had predicted to Abberline when the Ripper would cease to be active, and he was correct; but could it be that he had unwittingly told the Ripper himself when his time was up? Pride, if not a decisively more terrible motive, had previously prevented Abberline from consulting Sherlock Holmes; now at least, he could afford no pretences, and Holmes would be involved from the start.

'We shall really have to apologise to Mrs. Hudson for all of today's intrusions upon her. Ah, Lestrade, Inspector Abberline, to what do we owe such an untimely visit?' said Holmes, standing by the window as the two Inspectors came bustling loudly and unannounced through the door.

Inspector Abberline stood at a commanding six feet, his features sharp and intuitive: his almost entirely white hair seemed to be made of a single piece, originating from the scalp and encompassing his bushy whiskers before completing the circular effect in the form of a large moustache. He wore a conservative tweed suit with accompanying travellers coat and a black bowler hat. His demeanour was curt and irritable.

'Now is not the time for your snide remarks, Mr. Holmes,' he barked, striding purposefully into the centre of the room. 'A man of your intellect will undoubtedly be fully aware why Lestrade and myself have come to you at such an hour, and I assure you it is not to be on the end of your condescension! It is an unpleasant business, gentlemen, as I am sure you remember. But it may intrigue you most of all, Mr. Holmes, to learn that we have hit a bit of an unusual snag. The victim is, I am told, undoubtedly one of the Ripper's, but according to our men, it has not followed the previous progression.'

'Indeed you do intrigue me, Inspector. Pray, how does the victim differ from the previous?'

'As to that I cannot say, Mr. Holmes, we have not seen the body yet. I received this message from Constable Warrington:

'A girl has been murdered. Evidence suggests she is a victim of Jack the Ripper, though not conclusive. The body was found in the entrance to Deal Street Church; Dr. Phillips is on his way; bring Sherlock Holmes.'

'But how an earth does he know of Holmes' return?' I enquired.

'That was my doing, Dr. Watson,' Lestrade replied. 'I needed a few men for our earlier work. Warrington was eager to come, and I to have him with me, but H. Division claimed they needed him more urgently in Whitechapel.'

'Well, at least he has demonstrated sound judgment and sought my consultation from the off,' said Holmes, replacing his dressing gown with a travelling coat. 'An astute fellow, I am sure.'

'Now is not the time for your comments, Mr. Holmes, no matter how much truth they may or may not contain,' Abberline retorted bitterly.

'Our transport is downstairs, gentlemen,' said Lestrade, who had wisely chosen to remain neutral in the verbal sparring between his two superiors. 'Doctor, if you wish to remain behind and not be party to this terrible ordeal, we will of course understand.'

'If this demon has indeed returned, there are few men more than I who wish to see him banished back into the depths of hell,' I replied.

'Very well, I did not believe you would remain on the backbenches for this one.'

'I was unaware we were searching for Jack the Ripper in a library?' sneered Inspector Abberline, as Holmes collected a rather fine volume from one of the shelves. The book he held was one I had seen on several occasions: it was a quarto volume bound in deep burgundy Morocco with a large gilded 'M' emblazed upon the front cover. The paper was of high quality, and it was the only item in Holmes's chronicles that he had scribed himself: though sublime in detail, the others were closer in resemblance to scrap books. 'What the devil is that anyway?'

'This, Abberline, is my personal little tribute to the late Professor James Moriarty,' said Holmes.

'You may have been right about this Professor of yours while he still breathed among us, Mr. Holmes,' said Abberline, 'but I cannot entertain any superstitious nonsense that you believe him to have returned from beyond the grave.'

'Professor Moriarty was an exceptional criminal with an intellect of the first order, Inspector, but not even he is capable of resurrection. We are bringing the volume to refresh our memories of Jack the Ripper's previous activities. In this instance, it is the crime, not the man, in which we are interested.'

'So you can be mistaken after all,' retorted Abberline.

'On occasion, though if you should ask me to refrain from unhelpful comments, I must really ask for you to grant me the same courtesy. Now come, gentlemen, we have not a moment to spare; we shall re-familiarise ourselves with this most disturbing of cases upon the way.'

A bitter chill remained in the still night air as we entered the police carriage. Although drops had yet to fall, it seemed rain was not too distant, a fact which Holmes made quite clear to our driver. Our destination was a church upon Hanbury Street, situated upon the corner of Deal Street and King Edward Street. It is Holmes's usual custom under such circumstances to remain in a silent and meditative concentration, and though my mind was swimming with curiosity, I learnt long ago not to disturb him in such a state. Tonight though, he was insistent upon reliving that most disturbing of periods, and it was a task which I performed with the utmost reluctance.

'We are all familiar with the details. Do we have to go over them again?' said Lestrade.

'It is quite necessary, Lestrade, for we need our minds refreshed of all the minutiae; we must ensure we are aware of the repetition of any singularity or anomaly, otherwise our knowledge would be insufficient to tackle the case. If we were to be guilty of missing such a detail through our own idleness or reluctance to perform our duties, we should never have taken up a profession in detection.'

'He's right, Lestrade,' said Abberline, staring intently at Holmes.

'Please, Watson, I believe if you turn to page eighty, you will find the beginning to this most distasteful of chapters,' said Holmes, handing me his file upon the late Professor Moriarty.

'Friday, August 31, 1888, the body of Mary Anne (Polly) Nichols was found at three-forty in the morning.'

'Polly Nichols?' interjected Abberline. 'Holmes told you to start from the beginning, Dr. Watson; you have missed out the case of Martha Tabram.'

'I am afraid I do not concur with your conclusions regarding Miss Tabram, Inspector,' said Holmes.

'Do not concur? She was stabbed thirty-nine times, man!'

'Stabbed, Inspector, not ripped. Her throat was not cut, her carotid arteries left un-severed and her abdomen certainly not mutilated. Tragic and disturbing though her murder may have been, we shall not be accounting for her circumstances in our investigation. Should you wish to pursue such an end, you are of, course, at liberty; but now, Watson, I believe we last heard Miss Nichols was discovered at three-forty.'

'The body was discovered in the entrance to a stable yard,' I continued, 'found upon the northern end of Bucks-Row, heading toward Bakers-Row. She was discovered by a cabbie, Mr. Charles Cross, of twenty-two Doveton Street, Cambridge Heath Road, Bethnal Green. Nichols was no more than five feet and three inches; she had greying dark hair and a dark complexion. She was believed to be around forty-two years of age. Her clothing contained no features of interest, but on her person she carried a comb, a piece of looking-glass and a white pocket-handkerchief. There was no sign of a struggle. But two bruises were found on the right lower jaw and also the left cheek. Her throat had been slit twice, from left to right. The weapon was a moderately sharp, long-bladed knife. The windpipe, gullet and spinal cord had been severed.'

'Honestly, tonight is going to be disturbing enough! I have no problem recalling such details, and have been hard pressed trying to forget them!' cried Lestrade.

'Lestrade, if you cannot bear to hear what you have already seen, then perhaps you should not witness that which awaits us,' replied Holmes coldly, as Lestrade shrank back into his seat, a mutinous look across his brow.

'Further incisions were made to the abdomen,' I continued, 'notable for their depth and jagged nature. The genitalia suffered two small stab wounds. The victim died where she was found. The murderer had demonstrated anatomical knowledge.'

'With haste, driver,' demanded Holmes. 'Please Watson, continue your narrative.'

'Annie Chapman, alias 'Dark Annie', was found murdered on Saturday the eighth of September, at six o'clock. She was discoveredthree or four hundred yards from her dwellings, in the backyard of 29 Hanbury Street, Spitalfields, by John Davis. She was five feet tall and stoutly built, with dark brown hair and blue eyes. She was forty-seven years of age. Near the victim lay a piece of coarse muslin, a small tooth-comb and a pocket-comb in a paper case. There was no sign of a struggle. Miss Chapman's throat had been deeply cut, from left to right. Found above her right shoulder were her small intestines and a flap of abdomen, another section of which was placed by her left shoulder. Her skirt had been raised. Part of the belly, the womb and upper genitalia had been removed and were reported missing. Evidence suggested the murder took place in the courtyard, where a box of nails, a piece of flat steel and a saturated leather apron were also found. This discovery was attributed to the already suspected 'leather apron', real name Jack Pizer, a known prostitute abuser. No further or conclusive evidence could be brought against this unsavoury character.'

'If Dr. Phillips' testimony is included in that file, Dr. Watson, I should like to hear it,' injected Abberline.

'Dr. Phillips later gave evidence,' said I, flicking through the pages, 'that the weapon in question was a small amputating knife: narrow, sharp, and thin, around six to eight inches in length. He stated that 'no unskilled man could have carried out these operations. I myself could not have performed all the injuries, even without a struggle, in under quarter of an hour'

'Make a note for me to strike that from the account, Watson,' said Holmes. 'Why I thought Dr. Phillips' incompetence in comparison to Jack the Ripper was noteworthy, I cannot recall.'

'Dr. Phillips has been a police surgeon for over thirty years, Mr. Holmes. His opinion is held in the highest regard, and to make such a comment in comparison to this fiend is borderline slander!' cried Abberline.

'I do not question Dr. Phillips' ability or integrity Inspector Abberline, but is it really of surprise that Jack the Ripper possesses greater skill? So far he has committed these atrocities, despite being pursued by the police, myself and Watson, as well as having the entire public upon the lookout for him: yet he still roams free, lurking in the shadows. That he is more accomplished than Dr. Phillips is therefore of no surprise at all, Inspector Abberline, and I implore you not to waste anymore of our time with the pointless defence of one your colleagues. Now, so long as you have no more trivial remarks, please allow Watson to continue.'

'The night of the double murder,' said I, noting the look of pure fury upon the face of Inspector Abberline, 'Sunday the thirtieth of September, the body of Elizabeth Stride was discovered in Dutfield's Yard, Berner Street. She was discovered by Louis Diemshutz, the steward of the International Working Men's Educational Club. Miss Stride was five feet and five inches tall: she had a pale complexion, dark brown hair and light grey eyes. She was forty-five years of age. In her left hand she carried a packet of cachous. She was discovered lying face down; her throat deeply cut from left to right. Some authorities wished to dismiss this victim as the Ripper, but the technique used to cut the throat, as well as the body still being warm upon discovery, suggests she would have been subjected to mutilation and disembowelment had the Ripper not been interrupted. This theory is compounded by the discovery of Catherine 'Kate' Eddowes, later that same evening at a-quarter-to-two in Mitre Square: notable as the singular 'respectable' scene. Miss Eddowes was five feet tall, with dark auburn hair and hazel eyes. She was forty-six years of age. Upon her person were a small metal button, a common metal thimble and a mustard tin containing two pawn-tickets. There was no evidence of a struggle. Miss Eddowes was found upon her back, her clothes drawn up to the abdomen. Her throat was cut from left to right. Her face greatly disfigured. The majority of her intestines were placed over her right shoulder, a piece of which, approximately two feet in length, was detached and placed between the body and the left arm. The Ripper fled with Miss Eddowes's left kidney and womb. The execution showed less evidence of medical expertise than previous crimes, though I believe this to have been intentional.'

I paused in my narrative to contemplate the facts so far. None of the victims showed any sign of a struggle; although considering their occupation and that they were most likely to have been ambushed, this is hardly of surprise. It is also a safe assumption that Holmes would have made note of every detail that he believed to be of importance; the curious items found upon the bodies were therefore worthy of his attention, although I could not deduce any reason for being so.

'Could we have the latter stage of that particular night, please, Watson,' said Holmes, who seemed so vacant in his tone that I began to wonder whether it was the details themselves that he wished for, or rather a distraction from the irritation of Inspector Abberline.

'The murder of Miss Eddowes took place under the noses of no less than four serving or ex-policemen. Later that night at five minutes to three, Constable Alfred Long discovered a piece of a woman's apron stained with blood upon the staircase entrance to numbers 108-119, Wentworth Mouldings, Goulston Street. The apron later proved to be that of Miss Eddowes, and written upon the wall above in white chalk were the words:

'The Juwes are
The men That
Will not
Be blamed
For nothing.'

'On the premise of preventing an anti-Semitic riot, these words were removed at the order of Sir Charles

Warren, then Chief Commissioner of the Metropolitan Police. The evidence of the apron was left as a mocking token that not only had the Ripper claimed two victims in a single night, but he had also escaped the City boundary back into Whitechapel, undetected. The cryptic message upon the wall was believed to be deliberately misleading.'

'And now, gentlemen, we should have ample time to hear what was previously the final and most grotesque chapter in this most heinous of tales,' said Holmes.

'Friday the ninth of November, the body of Mary Jane Kelly was discovered in her lodgings at 3 Millers-Court. She was discovered by her landlord's shop assistant, at a-quarter-to-eleven in the morning. She was five feet and seven inches tall: she had a fair complexion, blonde hair and blue eyes. To those who are concerned by such matters, she was thought of as desirable. She was twenty-five years of age. There was no evidence of a struggle. Miss Kelly was found lying naked upon her bed. Her face had been butchered beyond recognition. Due to the extent of the lacerations, it was impossible to ascertain from which angle the throat had been cut. Her arms had been mutilated: her breasts removed. Beneath the head was the uterus, the kidneys and one breast, the other lay by her right foot. Situated between her feet was her liver. The intestines were placed upon the right side of her body: the spleen alongside the left. Upon the bedside table lay flaps removed from the abdomen and the thighs. A fire had been lit before the murder, and Kelly's clothes had been burnt to provide the Ripper with sufficient light.'

'Thank you, Watson,' said Holmes, turning his attention back inside the carriage. 'Now gentlemen, to briefly summarise all that we have heard,there is nothing remarkable about any of these crimes.'

'Holmes!' I shouted in unison with the two Inspectors.

'Let me rephrase,' said he, ever dramatic, and seemingly rather pleased with our indignant response. 'Other than the brutal nature in which these crimes were performed, they are by all accounts pointless slaughters with what would appear to be little motive; but it is the motive which we must focus upon. The victims have all been women of the night, but to mutilate them in such a fashion would suggest the Ripper is not primarily motivated by any perverted sense of moral cleansing; he is no demonic philanthropist. If this were so, then quantity would be key, not savage mutilation. The increasing ferocity of the crimes, accompanied with the evidence of his grotesque appetite not being satisfied upon the night of the double murder, is sufficient to support such a theory. I also do not believe these to be motivated in any way by any form of cult ritual. The only hypothesis we can follow is that he is motivated by terror and quenching his own perverse pleasure.'

'Savage!' spat Lestrade.

'It would be unwise to harbour such prejudices, Lestrade,' Holmes replied. 'Difficult though it is, we must try to remain emotionally unengaged in all cases. The atrocities Jack the Ripper has committed are adequate to blind any man with contemptuous rage, but we must keep him from pulling the blood-soaked wool over our eyes, and look only at the facts.'

'And which facts do you consider noteworthy, Mr. Holmes?' said Abberline.

'They are thus: he strikes always between twelve and six in the morning and always upon a weekend; his victims are always women, and more specifically, nightwalkers. He always uses a knife, with great skill and increasingly terrible violence. Each murder has left only the slightest trace of evidence, and is never sufficient to guide us down the correct path. His actions and continuing freedom suggest that he is a ruthless man with a meticulous logic and an education of the highest order.'

'Not unlike yourself then, Mr. Holmes,' Abberline sneered.

'In some respects, no,' he replied. 'We must remain careful, gentlemen, be mindful of these facts, but do not let them prejudice your judgment when we arrive. If we begin to theorise before we have the facts, we shall be forever chasing shadows through the underworld. I suggest we attempt to move our minds away from this ghastly business until we have the misfortune to examine the next victim of Jack the Ripper.'

As we reached our destination, I was struck by the location; although not a main-street, the murder had taken place on what was seemingly a busy road. Leading from this were side-streets and the darkest of alleyways, yet the murder was almost semi-public; the Ripper was moving out of the shadows. We were met at our carriage by a tall and powerful looking constable, and instantly one was struck by a commendable sense of purpose. I had heard Holmes mention Constable Warrington from time-to-time, and though they had yet to be formally introduced, he had gained a high reputation with both Holmes and the force. Despite his youth, the constable's strong personality accompanied by the occasional demonstration of reckless bravery had gained him a respect which far outstripped his rank. There was no man more befitting such a daunting task, but even this most valiant of fellows bore the visible disturbance of one who has only recently laid his eyes for the first time upon a victim of Jack the Ripper.

'Constable Warrington, I presume?' said Sherlock Holmes as we vacated the carriage.

'Mr. Holmes, it is indeed an honour sir,' said Warrington, wringing Holmes's hand.

'Constable,' interrupted Abberline, striding menacingly up to Warrington and standing so close to him that he could surely see his pupils dilate, 'let me make it clear to you right now; you do not give me orders. You do not tell me how to conduct my investigations; and, no-matter what childish admiration you have for Mr. Holmes, you do not decide whether I consult him. Unless, that is, you wish me to send you heroically on your own after a suspect in a rather unforgiving part of the city? Have I made myself clear?'

'I apologise, Inspector Abberline,' replied Warrington. 'It is the first time I have seen a victim of Jack the Ripper… I was not myself.'

We left Constable Warrington to continue his patrol of the area; the thought of a peacefully sleeping public was of slight comfort, but it would not be long before the brief interlude of docility would inevitably turn to widespread panic. Warrington's efficiency at least spared us any untoward local attention, but the distinct lack of human presence served only to create a more daunting atmosphere.

Some of our more fanciful newspapers may write of Britain and her glorious empire, but this is far from the complete picture; deep within the heart of this greatest of civilisations lies pockets of cancerous tumours. For every grand country home there is an urban slum: families living in basements, with filth and squalor as their homely companions. For these poor souls, the miracle of birth and the tragedy of death take place in the same room. Too often are the bright eyes of innocence opened, only to stare into the lifeless pits of a recently deceased loved one. The streets echo with the groaning of decay, and the nostrils burn at the stench of diseased and decomposing flesh. To a man of conscience, such suffering is a torture to behold: the glorious empire and her rotting children is a notion which is inconceivably immoral. I am not sure which disgusts me more, the existence of such conditions, or the wealthier elements of society who find themselves wandering into such areas, simply to leer at the residents as though they were some form of hellish circus.

Fortunately, tonight we would be spared the presence of those who saw the streets of Whitechapel as a walking tour of Bedlam. Other than the sounds of our boots upon the pavement, the streets were silent and empty: the rows of identical, inadequate houses were all blacked out, as if the presence of the Ripper had swept through, extinguishing all life within.

As we approached our destination, I glanced up to see the cold stone-grey of the church dominating my vision; the soft menacing glow of industrial furnaces caused the night sky to burn with a subdued yet furious anger. Though we approached a house of God, I was overcome with an intense feeling of foreboding: it was if the comfort of the Deity had been banished, and only the empty chill of evil remained. The grounds were surrounded by a stone wall, and though designed for privacy, they now served to contain the malevolent presence inside. We reached a breach in the form of an arch and a small wooden gate, where Dr. Phillips was awaiting our arrival.

'Mr. Holmes,' he said, as we approached. 'I must say that I am pleased to see you again, having read of your demise. But I was rather hoping to never lay eyes upon you again under professional circumstances.'

Despite Holmes's rather brisk reaction to Dr. Phillips

testimony, he was a much-liked and respected police surgeon. He was a charming man, and distinctly old-fashioned in both appearance and attire.

'Ah, Dr Phillips, I am inclined to agree with your sentiment. Within the confines of our profession, you are the last person I wish to see,' said Holmes.'

'And for good reason sir. If you gentlemen would please follow me, I shall escort you to the poor woman.'

A short loose-stoned path brought us before an alcove two yards in depth, a large wooden door at its end. Protruding from the left-hand side of the stone archway, which had been barely visible from the roadside, were two legs. Though I was braced for the horror which waited, I still recoiled at the sight. Slumped in the doorway was the body of a naked mutilated woman. Her skin was torn and ripped, her torso defiled, and her eyes removed. Though I had often noted Holmes's mechanical nature, I have never been more agitated by his complete lack of compassion.

'Could you please provide us with your report Dr. Phillips?' he said.

'Certainly; I shall give you a complete summary of the facts, and I think you will notice a few peculiarities.'

'I have already observed several, but pray proceed, and then we may compare our findings.'

'The victim has been dead for about two hours, placing the time of death around half-past two this morning. The woman is believed to have been in her mid-to-late-thirties. Her hair was removed prior to the murder. The throat has been slit from left to right. It is a relatively deep cut but sufficient only to kill the victim; it is not as deep as in previous instances. The face has been meticulously cut, but it has not been mutilated as we have seen before. The eyes have been expertly removed: a thin surgical blade was used for this part of the operation, and has been performed with professional execution. The victim has not been disembowelled, but the arms, legs and torso have been subjected to mutilation. The blade was inserted by about half-an-inch and dragged up the body, creating relatively deep, jagged columns. Upon the right hand only, all the fingers and the thumb have once again been expertly removed.'

'Is that all?' asked Holmes.

'Yes sir, although it is also notable that the victim had some very faint markings upon her wrists and ankles. Whether that is relevant or just an unfortunate result of her profession, I cannot say.'

'Well, that should be easy enough to deduce,' said Holmes, bending down to minutely examine the victim. 'She has not been moved? She was found slumped in this seated position, in this very alcove?'

'Yes sir, no one has moved the body.'

'Lestrade do you have a pencil upon your person? And Dr. Phillips, could I procure a swab?'

Gently using the offered pencil, Holmes lifted the lips of the victim in order to examine both her teeth and gums. He then took a sample of moisture from the woman's lips. Satisfied with the results, he handed the swab back to Dr. Phillips before examining every inch of the alcove and the church door. As Holmes walked off to examine the shingle path and surrounding area, I examined the body myself, but could note no omission on behalf of Holmes or Dr. Phillips, and simply stared into those empty sockets in disbelief that such horror had returned once more.

'Any theories, Holmes?' I enquired as he returned to the church entrance once more.

'Six so far, but none which are conclusive. The path

has been completely distorted by numerous prints, and so effectively obscures our murderer's print. This is undoubtedly one reason he chose the location. There are clear markings upon the street, which suggest a carriage drew up, stopped, and then departed. Such evidence suggests that the victim was chosen; brought to the location, and then subjected to these heinous crimes, to ensure that we would be certain of the man we are dealing with. I have sent Constable Warrington to fetch the man who discovered the body. Unfortunately, in a moment of ill-advised compassion, they allowed him to leave until called upon; we must hope he does not know of anyone in the area who can provide him with any form of medicinal comfort, or we shall be most inconvenienced.'

'Mr. Holmes,' said Constable Warrington, returning after a brief interlude, 'this is the man who discovered the victim, Mr. William Faulker.'

Before us stood a scruffy man of unfortunate circumstance: his clothing was frayed, his dark hair unkempt, and an aged cap perched carelessly on his head. His dirty face showed signs of poverty and also betrayed a hint of violence; though physically not a powerful man, his stocky frame suggested a strength which most would find surprising.

'It is a pleasure to make your acquaintance, Mr. Holmes,' said Mr. Faulker, an air of uncertainty in his otherwise gravelly voice.

'And yours, Mr. Faulker,' replied Holmes politely. 'I trust you have not consumed any substance that may have rendered you incapable of aiding us in our investigation?'

'No, sir. I most certainly wanted to but I cannot afford such luxuries.'

'I regret to hear of your troubles, Mr. Faulker, and I

sympathise with the distress you have suffered, nonetheless I am pleased you have remained sober. Fortunately I have brought with me a small flask of Watson's gin. Please take a mouthful to help regain your nerve, and if you would be so kind, describe for us how it was you came across this most unpleasant of scenes.'

'Thank you,' said Faulker, taking the flask, 'I live on Court Street, near the station, with my wife Marie and our three children.' He took a brief pause and a swig; it was unclear whether it was the effect of alcohol or the disturbing events of the night which caused him to shudder. 'Our circumstances are dire, but for around these parts that is regular,' he continued. 'I'm an Ale Turner at the brewery, on the east end of Pelham Street. Every morning I leave the house by four, walk up Hanbury Street, past this church, then go up Deal Street and onto Pelham. I saw the body lying in the entrance as I walked past.'

'That is your complete statement, Mr.Faulker?' said Holmes.

'Yes, sir, it is,' he replied gruffly.

'If that is indeed your entire statement, Mr.Faulker, then I assume you are hoping that I would fail to take into account the singularity that it was you in particular who discovered the victim, despite the numerous early risers who travel down this street? You wish me to ignore that the wall which surrounds these grounds obstructs the view of this alcove from every angle, and that the victim could only have been viewed from the gateway entrance? Even from there, this would prove exceedingly difficult: no mere passer-by could simply have noticed her out of the corner of their eye. Not only this, but also you wish me to ignore that, while you stood in this singular spot, you were also capable of noticing the woman's legs, which only slightly protruded from their area of shadowed concealment? You have also revealed, Mr. Faulker, that you live upon Court Street, which is remarkably close to where Polly Nichols was found murdered six years ago. Perhaps then, you are a far more sinister individual than Constable Warrington appreciated: after all, you could quite simply sink back into the shadows of your profession or your establishment, having carried out such deeds. If I were you, Mr. Faulker, I would provide a more coherent case for your discovery, or you shall find yourself placed amongst the most infamous of suspect lists: that of Jack the Ripper.'

Our man had turned a ghostly shade of white as he realised his miscalculation. His breathing became sharp and his hands began to tremble; it seemed as if he were about to embark upon some form of grotesque transformation.

'Mr. Holmes, I assure you that I am not capable of such violence,' Faulker stammered.

'Once again, Mr. Faulker, I must insist that you stick to the facts.'

'You accuse me of such a crime?'

'I do not accuse you of anything: I can see by the scratches upon your neck, the rips in your clothing, and your slightly bleeding knuckles that you have been involved in a recent skirmish. Furthermore, we have a dead woman, and a highly suspicious and, judging by your countenance at my remarks, violent individual, who is refusing to or incapable of providing an adequate alibi as to how he discovered the victim. Perhaps you thought you would be clever and avoid suspicion by alerting the authorities yourself? So I ask you again, Mr. Faulker, how did you discover this woman?'

'Very well,' said he, his face in a state of terrible

contortion. 'There are some things a man wishes to remain private, even from the authorities. I told you I have three children, Mr. Holmes, but a little over two weeks ago, I had four. Our youngest and my only daughter, Emily, was just two years old, but she contracted some awful disease and died within days. I attend this church regularly but it has no cemetery, at least not for people of my background. Emily was buried in one of those great cemeteries outside the City; but every day, upon my way to work, I stop for a few minutes at the gate and say a prayer for my baby daughter. I wouldn't have noticed the body, but there was a bit of a breeze and it made her dress blow about her ankle. I thought the movement was a bit odd, and when I strained, I thought I saw what looked like legs. I went to have a look and then alerted the authorities.'

'The death of an infant is not uncommon, Mr. Faulker. Why is it that you wish me to believe a man such as yourself would harbour such sentiment?'

'Whatever you comfortable folk may believe about the citizens who make up the bulk of this city, we are not savages. The death of one of your own is a pain no man, no matter what his circumstances, should be made to suffer. Not that I would expect you to understand.'

'A touching story, Mr. Faulker,' said Holmes, 'I thank you for giving us the true and complete version of your night's events. If you have nothing more to add, you may continue upon your way.'

'Holmes, I understand you wish to extract the truth but must you use such tactics?' said Abberline, as William Faulker departed the scene, an array of pain and emotion evident in his eyes.

'Had he not insisted upon providing an incomplete testimony I would not have pushed him so; if he had presented before us the complete narrative when I first enquired, I would have been inclined to believe him and prepared to have been more sympathetic.'

'A coherent account, I would say, but should we not have asked him about the carriage?' said Lestrade.

'No, the murder took place hours before the body was discovered by Mr. Faulker. Jack the Ripper vanishes into the shadows, he does not sit in a carriage waiting to be sighted. As for my suspicion of the man, I never believed in his guilt; such people mistrust the authorities and are always reluctant to give a full account, even though it usually contains nothing incriminating, they merely gain satisfaction from being unhelpful. In such circumstances, demonstrating the stupidity of such action is usually sufficient, in this case more than so. What conclusions did you draw upon your inspection of the body, Watson?'

'The teeth and gums are quite healthy, and the fingernails appear well kept. The skin looks a little off-colour, though, something which could have only developed over time, so I assume you were searching for traces of poison. I also noticed that the wounds around the fingers and the eyes have been wiped; the excess blood was smeared across the door and upon the handle, but the neck and torso were left alone, though I can offer no reason for this action.'

'Excellent. I had deduced as much. As for the poison, the evidence would suggest such a method, though at this stage of the investigation I cannot be certain. So, gentlemen: we have heard from our man, and seen the body, do any theories begin to materialise?'

'The fingers and mouth surely point to a life of relative comfort,' said Inspector Abberline.

'Perhaps, although not necessarily,' said Holmes. 'Watson?'

'The nails were well kept but slightly soiled; that is suggestive of one who took pride in her appearance but did not have the means to do so, or her circumstance dictated that she at least must dirty her hands. She could had previously lived in comfort and recently fallen on hard times.'

'Excellent, Watson! I would be inclined to use your theory as the basis for one of our more probable hypotheses. If we apply the same reasoning to a similar train of thought, we may also consider the possibility that she was a lady of the night who was being courted by a wealthy benefactor. Such a scenario is quite common, and I am told that a number of women get into the profession in the hope of achieving such an end.'

'And if she had been poisoned and brought to the scene?' injected Lestrade.

'Bravo Lestrade, you focus upon the two notable features of the case. She was certainly brought here by carriage, and the likelihood of poison, in tandem with the marks upon her wrists and ankles, suggests she had been held captive. The victim, as you perceive, gentlemen, is an anomaly.

'And the fingers?' I asked.

'For one of either two plausible reasons:the fingers and thumb were removed from the right hand only, so naturally it was upon this hand which she wore items of value or recognition.'

'Are we sure this is the Ripper?' said Abberline. 'All the previous murders appeared to be random. We had no trouble identifying any of the victims and found no motive, other than increasingly devilish violence. Now you are saying that the same man purposefully kept a woman hostage, poisoned her, removed her identifiable features and cleaned only some of the wounds, before smearing her blood upon a church door?'

'We have an anomaly,' repeated Holmes. 'The public location accompanied with the slitting of the throat, the unnecessary rips along the body, as well as the demonstration of expertise in the delicate removal of the eyes and the fingers, show that this is no mere impersonator. As for the smearing of the blood, I can only assume that defiling a house of God would appeal to such a man; not every action has a devious purpose, Abberline. We have but one similarity to our previous victims; we have been left with what I believe to be purposefully insufficient evidence. Our working hypothesis is thus: Jack the Ripper has kidnapped and murdered a woman believed to have been, or becoming, of reasonable status; he bound her, and to free himself of the duties of watchman used a slow-working poison. When it became apparent that she would not fulfil his original design, he brought her to this church and carried out these atrocities, though why I cannot say.'

'We shall alert the Yard to begin a search for such a woman straight away,' said Lestrade.

'Anything else?' asked Abberline.

'Yes, search for any men who are also teetering between social escalation and disaster, with possibly a wife or daughter who has gone missing.'

'What about the wealthy clients of these women, Holmes?' said I. 'If she were looked after, she could bear the appearance of a woman of higher class.'

'A solid theory Watson, and one which we shall pursue; the authorities are unlikely to have much luck enquiring into such personal matters, and I believe they would be met with blunt and rather unhelpful responses. We shall use more unofficial means directed at the social associates of the woman.'

'But do we not have any leads as to the identity of this

man,' exclaimed Lestrade, a hint of desperation in his voice.

'Unfortunately not, Lestrade, for we are hunting Jack the Ripper. The man we chase is an anonymous spectre; he may well even be dead. There is little more for us to learn here gentlemen. Watson and I shall return to Baker Street and await any further developments, for until we discover the identity of this poor woman, we have reached an impasse.'

# 7

# A GREAT DECEPTION

IT WOULD PERHAPS be a trifle inaccurate to describe the following days as panic-stricken: they were sheer pandemonium. Never in my life had I seen such terror. One would think that an announcement had been issued for some ghastly European war. The press, of course, revelled in delight, and not a second was wasted before the sensationalism of murder was blazed across what seemed to be every publication: hundreds of pages of lurid and graphic descriptions were upon the tips of almost every tongue. Newsboys shouted their usual distasteful slogans at passers-by:

'Resurrection of the Ripper: new murder in Whitechapel!'

'Back from Hell: woman Ripped outside of church!'

The public, though horrified at the crimes, had no issue with devouring every sentence, listening to every fairytale, and gossiping in the streets over the identity of this most infamous of criminals. It was not until I journeyed around some of London's more civilised quarters that I began to feel cold, suspicious eyes upon me. I heard the faintest of whispers, similar to a gentle yet unnerving breeze upon a cool dark night, rustling menacingly through the leaves of dying trees: soft mutterings, terrified murmurs which haunted my every step. The more intellectual sections of society had noted a rather curious trend in recent events; the rise, fall and resurrection of Jack the Ripper was an almost perfect reflection of my companion's recent activities. Sherlock Holmes, the foremost champion of the law, the pinnacle of reason, had become a Ripper suspect. Of course, such notions were utterly contemptible. Myself, Lestrade and two other constables were with him throughout the night of the recent murder, with myself and Mrs. Hudson completing the alibi upon that day. But such is the nature of society that they are willing to believe any wild theory. My portraits of Holmes' abilities had created an image of such profound genius that some were willing to believe he could be in two places at once. Others believed that I was his accomplice.

I am sure those who harboured these suspicions felt vindicated, and were convinced that we were merely cowering from their accusations, when Holmes and I locked ourselves away in Baker Street: but I can assure you our self-imprisonment served a far greater purpose. For days, Holmes had been consumed by work. Measuring cylinders, glass test tubes and small Bunsen flames could be seen throughout our quarters, and often peculiar and most undesirable smells were to be found simmering within. At least a hundred samples of chemical substances lay scattered across our rooms. A great pile of unanswered correspondence sat upon the side-table, some of which I am sure presented the kind of intricate puzzles my friend would have previously relished the opportunity to investigate.

During this time, I decided that while I could not be of help to Holmes directly, I would at least be of some use;

certainly I had no desire to walk amongst those who suspected my involvement in such disturbing events. I therefore decided to analyse those neglected suspects, on the albeit highly unlikely premise that the official authorities had in fact been upon the true course. They may have been previously dismissed, but it was necessary to determine the plausibility of such men in relation to the development of recent events. It was clear to me that, though likely to fail, it was a necessary step, for Holmes could no longer insist upon his Moriarty theory.

My search began with a man named Montague John Druitt. In 1888, he was believed to be insane and suspected guilty by his own friends, with whom the police had been in contact. I immediately hit a dead-end, however, when I discovered he had committed suicide soon after the murder of Mary Jane Kelly. His suspicion was never taken seriously by most within the upper-echelons of the force, and was suspected rather flimsily by his companions; the only somewhat far-fetched conclusion, which had been placed upon such a suspicion, was that his suicide coincided with the final murder. This presented a rather simplistic yet tidy explanation for the end of the Ripper, but even amongst the most ludicrous of conspirators this could now be clearly dismissed.

My next suspect was a Polish Jew by the name of Aaron Kominski. He was labelled insane due to many years in solitary vices; he had a known hatred for women, as well as homicidal tendencies. I recall Lestrade mentioning that Kominski was of notable interest as he bore resemblance to the man seen in Mitre Square in the company of Catherine Eddowes. The suspect also lived in the immediate vicinity of the crimes, and some believed that due to the nature of the lower-Jewish class to which he belonged, his people refused to give up one of their own to Gentile justice. However, I could gather no evidence that this man had displayed even the rudimentary basics of anatomical knowledge. Mr. Kominski was admitted into a lunatic asylum in March 1891, but was discharged and moved to Leavesden Asylum near Watford on April 13, 1894, where he had remained ever since. Once again I had found myself staring down the barrel of defeat. There was no conceivable explanation how this man could have carried out the latest murder if he still resided in an asylum.

Determined to find something of interest to raise before Holmes, I examined the case of Michael Ostrog: a thief, confidence trickster and self-proclaimed doctor. He had been caught and prosecuted for numerous thefts before being admitted into Wandsworth Prison, a lunatic asylum in Surrey. He was discharged upon the tenth of March 1888, and three weeks after the double murder, an advert was placed in the *Police Gazette* with a description and caption that stated 'special attention is called to this dangerous man'. He was a man who had been recently discharged from a lunatic asylum, with anatomical knowledge and a known past for crime and cruelty to women.

'Ostrog could not bc placed at any of the previous scenes,' said Holmes.

I had scarcely noticed that he had risen from his chair, let alone was now leaning over my shoulder and examining my notes.

'I did not realise you had taken notice of these men.' said I, slightly flustered.

'I always give suspects a momentary glance, Watson, no matter how absurd they may appear. A fruitless and rather tedious task it is, but I must always ensure that every path is travelled when I am in the dark over my destination,' said he, taking a seat next to me.

'There are no previous suspects who arouse your attention then?'

'Only one,' said he.

'Holmes?'

'Professor James Moriarty.'

'What on earth would make you state such a fallacy? He could not possibly have committed the latest atrocity.'

'Look out into the streets, Watson. You have seen the panic, the terror; you have heard the whispers and rumours that surround us. Sherlock Holmes is Jack the Ripper and dear Watson, my ever-faithful accomplice. Who else could have conjured such a notion? Who else could have manipulated the public into swallowing such a deception? The more I consider the problem, the more I am convinced that this is all some terrible scheme which has been left behind. Perhaps Moriarty was not the Ripper after all, Watson, perhaps he merely orchestrated him. Take these suspects, for example; if we apply my hypothesis we could read the situation as thus: Moriarty hired or threatened Mr. Druitt to murder only Mary Jane Kelly. He had no connection with the previous victims, was recruited and then taught how to inflict such injuries. There was then a buffer in place, so that if Mr. Druitt began to show signs of moral fibre, the kind of remorse which would have disgusted Moriarty, he was disposed of into the Thames: one Jack the Ripper cast into the mighty river, made to appear as suicide. Both our next suspects could have also been the Ripper. Their insanity could have been caused by the atrocities they had committed, a means of escape from the murderous figure of Moriarty, or forced upon them by the Professor himself. One by one a different Jack the Ripper adds to the work of his predecessor, before being presented with quite the conundrum: a choice between insanity, suicide, or their own murder.

'Such an orchestration would certainly explain the force's inability to catch the man,' I said.

'Quite. Now, if you pass me your notes I think we shall find them of greater use than you may have anticipated.'

I passed Holmes my papers, bewildered at this most intriguing of developments. The rebirth of his Moriarty theory at first sounded like the ramblings of a lost soul, refusing to relinquish his grasp upon a singular strand of straw that had blown away so long ago; but as ever, Holmes's seemingly fanciful beginning appeared to be developing into the kind of circular theory he so often championed.

'Here we have Druitt. An Oxford man with a third-class degree in classics, he became a teacher before attempting a profession in law. He had a considerable social standing, and became Director of Blackheath Cricket Club. The years prior to his death were marred by tragedy: the death of his father and the incarceration of his mother in a mental institution say as much. But this does not strike me as the profile of a man upon the brink of suicide. The most suggestible piece of evidence was given by his brother, William, who claimed Montague had stated, 'I felt like I was going to be like mother, and the best thing for me was to die'. Suggestive, is it not?'

'You believe Moriarty was forcing him into a mental asylum, so he committed suicide?'

'It seems plausible, if he performed the deed himself; then at least he chose the manner in which he joined the afterlife, rather than waiting in fear for whatever terrible scheme Moriarty may have planned for him. The method would have been of irrelevance to Moriarty, so long as he achieved his desired result. Our next man, Kominski, was an unmarried hairdresser. There was no history of mental illness in his family, and the cause of the illness remains unknown.'

'I assume this fits into your Moriarty theory as well?' I enquired.

'Quite; either his mental instability was caused, as we have said, by performing such deeds or through the terror of Moriarty which still gripped his heart. Perhaps more likely was that the institution in which he was imprisoned had, and continues to have, an anonymous benefactor who ensures the man is supplied with suitable substances to maintain his condition. As for Mr. Ostrog, his early years were tarnished with countless cases of theft and identity fraud, and you mention in your notes, Watson, that he was committed into a lunatic asylum. But you failed to note that there were several present at his trial, PC Mulvey and Dr. Hillier for example, who believed he was trying to manipulate the court. Not exactly surprising behaviour from a confidence trickster, of course, but it is rather telling that Dr. Hillier stated that Ostrog showed no signs of insanity when he saw him at the police station. Curious then, how he was able to achieve admission, despite being under the light of suspicion. Of course, that the authorities failed to link the man satisfactorily with any of the crimes is neither here nor there if he were being orchestrated by Professor Moriarty.'

'What about the last victim? Perhaps this is the reason behind Moran's and Adair's clash?'

'That is a distinct possibility; after all, Moran is more than capable of such persuasion, while it is obvious that he would have laid such plans prior to his visit to the empty house. Perhaps Adair did finally discover his moral compass and was incapable of orchestrating such vicious crimes, necessitating the need for his immediate removal. But regardless, having examined some of the facts, does my theory bear scrutiny?'

'To an extent, Holmes,' said I, still slightly apprehensive, 'but it does not account for the fact that only one of these men can be placed at only one of the crime scenes. I know this does not disprove your theory, far from it if we are talking of Moriarty, but surely that will not be sufficient for the authorities?'

'I admit that as an official line of investigation it is for the time being rather inadequate; however, I may point to the fact that I encountered many such dead-ends during the majority of my pursuit of the Professor. To dismiss such a notion, when faced with an all-too-familiar continuity, would be a mistake which could well cost me my life, and indeed, perhaps even yours. We must be careful, my dear fellow, we are re-entering very dangerous waters. Our case may not be tight enough for the ears of Lestrade and Abberline at the present time, but I believe we at least are upon the correct path. Our attention must be focused toward any other plausible suspect who has taken a rather sudden and unexpected turn toward insanity or suicide. But for now, Watson, what I require of you is a task in which I am sure you will take great pleasure.'

'Holmes?'

'Do you recall my telling you that the press is a valuable institution, if you know how to use it?'

'I do,' said I, slightly bemused.

'Well, as Jack the Ripper is clearly using my own words against me, I rather believe it is time to retaliate. You are my press, Watson, and I need you to publish some more of your charming little narratives which romanticise yet to a large degree dilute my cases. You may consult my notes, though I must insist you enquire with me first as to their suitability for publishing, since there are still matters that must remain private. There should be plenty of accounts which satisfy your usual criteria, but should they prove lacking in fictional value, I am sure that together we can fabricate a suitable tale or two.'

'But why do you wish me to carry out such a task now? You have never allowed me unrestricted access to your notes before.'

'I need to continue my work uninterrupted, Watson; therefore you can search all my notes, but only enquire when something takes your fancy. I have no desire to carry out an unnecessarily tedious question and answer task. As for the stories, they will demonstrate that I have returned to business as usual, and Jack the Ripper will assume, quite rightly, that I cannot move until the identity of his latest victim is discovered. We must play the game, Watson. He wishes the public to turn against me, so I must return to business and infuriate them further still by openly demonstrating that my attention is elsewhere.'

'It seems an unnecessary risk to me, Holmes. Would it not be more beneficial to try and regain the confidence of the public?'

'As a rule, you are of course correct, but for now it is better that they believe I am at least active in my profession, rather than locked up in Baker Street with a chemistry set.'

It is with slight embarrassment, when one considers the events which had so recently occurred, that I confess the next few days were rather enjoyable. Holmes continued his exhaustive search for the substance upon the victim's lips: a task which would have been far simpler if he had an adequate sample. Fortunately, although the Ripper in his malevolent deviance had realised such a notion, he failed to sufficiently cleanse the victim's lips, and a small residue had been left upon the lower gum, providing Holmes with the smallest of traces. I, meanwhile, had the pleasure of taking to my pen and scribing some of my tales of old. There was 'The Case of the Black Diamond', 'The Adventure of the Puppet Master' and 'The Curious Incident of the Dog and the Bone'. I had concluded that, though these were not entirely devoid of interest, they were not up to my usual standard, and so I settled upon one rather intriguing case, 'The Adventure of the Norwood Builder.'

'How is our little press stunt coming along, Watson?' asked Holmes, still behind his array of smouldering tubes.

'I believe the narrative of the builder shall be an adequate tale,' I replied.

'Excellent. I had rather hoped that would take your fancy. I myself am rather fond of some of the puzzles and intricacies which the other tales contain; but I feel that your readers, who so mundanely insist upon the more superficial elements, would not be so impressed.'

We were interrupted at this juncture by a soft knocking at the door and the entrance of Mrs. Hudson, a thoroughly dishevelled look upon her motherly features.

'I hope you do not expect me to navigate such a labyrinth of obstacles simply to bring you your breakfast, gentlemen? Even a German would be daunted by such a task,' she said with an air of impertinence.

'Mrs. Hudson, of course I would not ask you to brave the treacherous environment we have created. Watson is no longer performing any noteworthy task, so I am sure he will oblige your request.'

'Thank you, Doctor,' said she, awaiting my assistance as I cast my narrative in Holmes's direction, 'but I must say, Mr. Holmes, I find it rather difficult to believe that Dr. Watson can be held responsible for such chaos.'

'You would find yourself rather surprised at what dear old Watson can be held accountable for,' said Holmes.

'He is joking, of course, Mrs. Hudson. He often finds it comforting to lower me to his standards,' I said, taking the tray from her hands and waiting for her to depart before turning back to Holmes. 'Must you try and make Mrs. Hudson regard me in the same manner in which she does you?'

'Don't be hysterical Watson.'

'You know you can perform some menial tasks yourself,' I replied, dropping the tray upon the table.

'If you can solve the mystery of this most illusive of substances, I would be more than happy to switch roles; but if memory serves me correctly, your expertise is in biology not chemistry, so I am afraid it is you who shall have to remain the wife in our relationship for the time being.'

'If you could use some other metaphor, Holmes it would be appreciated. Mary is not so easily forgotten,' I replied tearing open the day's paper, rather hurt by the callous and mechanical nature my friend could often display.

'I do apologise for my lack of tact, Watson. Is there any news in the morning paper?'

I admit that Holmes did not have my full attention, and his voice had become a rather distorted drone.

'Watson?' he repeated, impatiently.

'You have another correspondence from Jack the Ripper,' said I.

'Ah, I was getting worried he would forget to write. What does darling Jack have to share with me this time?'

'It reads as follows:

'Holmes has returned! Now it's all fair game,
But the girl's still Ripped, *oh what a shame.*
The corpses are rising and I have *my prize,*
He sits in a chair, thinks he's *so wise.*

You won't find me there, still I roam free,
Stay there too long, it'll turn into a spree.
I hear the people whisper, a case he can't crack?
Remembered forever...

*Outwitted by Jack.'*

'That is all?' said Holmes finally.

'That is all.'

'It would seem our little bluff has been called before we even had chance to play our hand. Nevertheless, it has been time well spent. The substance upon the lips of the victim was tartar emetic, a soluble white powder, which contains antimony. It is practically tasteless, odourless and colourless. In sufficient quantities, it would produce vomiting and exhaustion. If administered over a long enough period of time, it would cause an unsuspicious death, and most would believe the murder to have been caused by a far more commonplace illness. For Jack the Ripper, it is the perfect substance; it would weaken the hostage and prevent any form of unnecessary and tedious struggle.'

'I do not believe I have ever heard of such a substance,' said I, horrified at the further evil the Ripper was deploying.

'Few physicians have. But if we are to be certain of our findings, we must pay a visit to the mortuary.'

'The mortuary? But Holmes, it is a miracle you have managed to deduce what you have from such an inadequate sample, surely there will be none remaining by now.'

'Right you are,' said he, putting on his travelling coat, 'but there is one more unexpected side-effect such a substance has upon the body, and I will need your medical expertise to confirm my suspicions. We shall therefore first visit the mortuary before taking a rather unpleasant stroll around Whitechapel.'

'For what purpose?' said I, collecting our revolvers from the desk.

'We must play along with Jack for now. Clearly he wishes us to be out playing in the streets instead of locked away in our rooms. We may as well oblige him. We have no further cause for remaining in our lodgings, and if, by visiting the previous scenes, we conjure a distant memory or awaken a long forgotten instinct which throws us upon the path of enlightenment, it shall be a journey well spent.'

Though Holmes was not bothered by such slander, I had grown rather tired of some of the snarling remarks on the street regarding our supposed involvement in the crimes of the very man we continued to pursue; and so was grateful he had chosen to have a cab called prior to our departure from Baker Street.

We left the shelter of 221B swiftly, and as we rattled along in our carriage toward the East End, I spent the entire of our journey in a state of anxious curiosity, trying to anticipate what side-effect this mysterious compound could cause. The poison itself seemed to be such an ideal substance for the task at hand that it was difficult to imagine what traces it could possibly have left almost a week after the last dosage had been administered.

Since there is no public mortuary in Whitechapel, the body of our victim had been moved to a nearby workhouse infirmary upon Old Montague Street, which had a dead-house as part of its premises. Upon arrival, our view was dominated by a formidable sombre mass of grey stone. It was as if the building itself bore some of the psychological scars from the suffering that it contained. The arched windows were mere pockets of false-hope, admitting a light which could never inspire freedom into the hearts of the unfortunate souls who dwelled inside. Having found the entrance locked, we knocked firmly upon the large wooden door, and were unwelcomingly received by a rather crude and dishevelled-looking man.

Usually Holmes' status of consulting detective does not cause much of an issue, such is his reputation, but the cloud of suspicion which had begun to surround him in this dreadful business caused an unnecessary delay before we gained the information which we required. Upon our last visit to Old Montague Street, in 1888, the mortuary had been nothing more than an inadequately lit and unhygienic shed, but such had been the complaints that an improved, though still rather unkempt replacement, along with a new post-mortem area, had been constructed in the south-east corner of the premises.

We gained access via an entrance in Thomas Street, and were shown into a dark room where the scent of the deceased instantly took us by the throat. The room was lit sporadically by wall-mounted oil-lamps, and the ceiling was curved into a large arch, causing shadows to form grotesquely around the room. This small enclave was filled with bodies of the recently departed laid out upon wooden frames and hidden beneath featureless white cloaks: thin, indiscriminate veils which separated life from death.

Our host unfortunately did not know which of our anonymous collective would be the Ripper victim, although I scarcely imagined we would have trouble identifying her once we uncovered the correct veil. Holmes and I took a lamp each and set about our task of individually unmasking the dead. It was a most disturbing business. I pulled back one of the veils and found myself looking into eyes of a child who not so long ago could have been peacefully sleeping. She could have been dreaming of great adventures, sailing the many seas, running free and indulging in the many worldly fruits that can tantalise even the most pessimistic of minds. But now she had been mercilessly struck down, her once innocent features immersed into the lifeless stone, her playful laughter turned into silent screams.

'Here we are, Watson,' said Holmes. Although I was not altogether surprised at his tone of muffled amusement, I was still agitated that he could be so insufferable in such surroundings. Nothing, however, could prepare me for the shock that awaited.

'I know these suspicions are mere wives-tales, but you should really try to alter your usual manner, Holmes!' I cried in astonishment at the sight before me.

There stood Sherlock Holmes, his triumphant smile barely visible in the darkness as he held back the veil and shone his lamp upon the face of the deceased woman. The face of the victim looked almost identical to when I had last laid my eyes upon her. 'How can this be?'

'I believed that the substance I had found contained antimony, which I knew if consumed in sufficient quantities prior to death, prevents the decomposition of the flesh, preserving the body. I therefore must insist upon your medical expertise and ask whether you believe the victim was likely to have been subjected to such a substance prior to her murder?'

'Was this deception really necessary, Holmes? I was not expecting you to enjoy yourself so much upon this journey!'

'Jack is having his fun, Watson; am I not entitled to some amusement of my own?'

'I do not believe such behaviour is advisable, considering public suspicions. Do you really want murmurings to turn into outcry?'

'The public will believe whatever is printed in our gloriously *free* press. For the time being, we have no choice but to accept their naivety and gullibility; but don't worry, the time will come when they will look upon us favourably once more.'

'Forgive me for saying so, but you seem rather assured of yourself.'

'We have our facts and we have our poison. Once we discover the identity of our victim, I am sure all will begin to fit into place. You forget that after all, we are hunting a man, not a demon. Men can always be caught.'

It was clear to me, as it so often is, that Sherlock Holmes knew far more than he cared to divulge. In almost every case that I have had the privilege of sharing with him, rarely am I privy to the full extent of his theories until the very conclusion of our adventures: such is the life of befriending a brilliant mind, with an often irritating fondness for the theatrical. At least I could take comfort in the knowledge that the rest of our journey around Whitechapel, though distinctly unpleasant, would not contain any more of his ruses.

I had accompanied Holmes in these parts upon countless occasions, but I was always struck by the social imbalance, which people do not always associate with such areas. One moment, usually upon one of the main streets, you could be in an area of what appeared to be satisfactory living standards, but a single turn down one of the many narrow dark and menacing alleys, and you would soon be amongst the very dregs of society. Filth and deprivation spilled out into the overcrowded streets, creating the impression of one large social-cesspool.

Our journey was a relatively long and arduous one. Had it been determined by distance rather than by the chronology of the events, we would have been spared much time. However, Holmes insisted that we should not follow in the inept footsteps of our colleagues, but in the tracks of Jack the Ripper. Had our journey contained features of interest, I would present a much richer narrative, but to attempt such a claim would be an almost complete falsehood. It shall therefore suffice to scribe only the bare facts.

Every murder took place in a quiet and secluded part of the district, but only in the case of Mary Jane Kelly did the Ripper act in complete privacy. Mitre Square represented the only area of relative affluence. Only outside the church upon Deal Street was there any evidence of a carriage; for all other murders, the Ripper arrived on foot and then disappeared silently into the night.

Upon our return to Baker Street, Holmes entered our rooms in a fashion of marked irritability. Rarely had I seen him in such a state when distracted by the intellectual euphoria of a case.

'Lestrade has left us a message,' said I, noticing a piece of paper upon the table, which Holmes had rather uncharacteristically ignored.

'Is it yet further proof documenting his incompetence?' he barked.

'Along those lines, yes. It states:

'Dear Mr. Holmes, Inspector Abberline and I have been unsuccessful in locating or discovering any knowledge of a currently missing woman previously of a comfortable background and who has recently fallen upon hard times. Our enquiry into any men of similar circumstance, whose spouse might have disappeared, has also been unsuccessful. There has been no news of any woman of notable class or wealth who has been kidnapped within the last year, held for ransom or otherwise. We shall visit Baker Street soon to discuss our next course of action. Lestrade.'

'Yet more dead ends, Holmes. Were you ever confident that Lestrade and Abberline would be successful in such lines of enquiry?'

'We must investigate and eliminate all possibilities, otherwise we shall never be successful in our search for the truth. After all, someone *is* dead,' said he, spreading a large and intricately detailed map of London across the table before lighting up his pipe. 'There is nothing remarkable about any of the locations, Watson. Here, you see I have marked all the crime scenes, and there is nothing, not so much as a ritualistic symbol from an extinct civilisation. I have arranged all the letters of each address accordingly, and there is no hidden code, no secret, not even a childish riddle. There was previously a slight pattern which could be found in the measure in the dates between the murders, but now even that flimsiest of notions has been ripped from my hands. This anomaly is purely for the sake of being an anomaly. There is no logic, Watson!'

'Perhaps that is reason in itself?' I offered. 'That is the only conclusion the evidence suggests.'

'Only the murders suggest such a theory. You neglect his knowledge of my survival, as well as the rather crude and unsubtle taunts which travel beyond the white cliffs of our great shores and broadcast around the world that Sherlock Holmes is being beaten by a savage and his blade.'

'My dear Holmes, I know he taunts you but surely this is more complex than that? After all he did not communicate with you at all via any method, let alone public taunts, in 1888.'

'I cannot say. Moriarty wove a web of crime encompassing all of London: he played his game and I played mine. Jack the Ripper is not so easy. Was he Moriarty, or, as I am now inclined to believe, an orchestrated illusion? All we know now is, only after Moriarty's death and the return of Jack the Ripper does he care to taunt me; and not only this, but in a manner which suggests it was his motive all along. It does not add up.'

'Holmes, have you entertained the possibility that Moriarty is not involved in this whole affair at all? What if Jack the Ripper is truly a deranged yet unknown surgeon, who only dared mock you after his success and your supposed demise?'

'That is a possibility; you draw your conclusions firmly from the facts, but your theory neglects one crucial aspect: no mere slaughterer, no doctor with an imbalanced mind and murderous temperament could have known my suspicion of Moriarty. If you are correct and the complex riddle which I have spun is indeed far simpler, then I am afraid we have but one path available to us.'

'Inspector Abberline knew of your suspicions,' I offered.

'I know you are suspicious of the Inspector, and I admit your reasoning for being so is considerably less far-fetched than a lot of the woeful theories which emerge from Scotland Yard itself. We shall, of course, not rule out such a hypothesis, but I would not make it the focus of our investigation. If Abberline is indeed the Ripper that would be a most unfortunate development, but our course of action would not be altered. If we cannot discover the Ripper's identity through more conventional methods, we must revert back to the more crude option of catching him red-handed. Such a course of action is, as you appreciate, exceedingly difficult and almost certain to fail; but I begin to believe that we may be left with no other alternative. Should we fail, the most infamous criminal of our time will be allowed to sink back into the shadows.'

'That is no option for me; we must see him hanged!' I cried.

'I share your sentiments. Never has a man deserved the rope more, yet never has a man been further from such a fate, but I am afraid that unless our fortunes change, he may escape our grasp forever.'

'If you can rid the world of Professor Moriarty, Holmes, I am certain you can banish Jack the Ripper back into whichever dark realm he was spawned.'

'You flatter me, my dear fellow, but a spider and its web are always easier to locate than the solitary serpent.'

At this juncture, we were interrupted by the sound of uninvited official footsteps upon the stairs; but, to both our surprise, it was neither Lestrade nor Abberline coming to discuss the somewhat deteriorating situation. Instead we were greeted by a young constable: Smith was his name, and his eyes twinkled with an eagerness suggestive of inexperience.

'I beg your pardon, Mr. Holmes, Dr. Watson,' said he, a slight quiver in his attempted impression at authority, 'but I was told not to waste a second by Chief Inspector Abberline and Inspector Lestrade. They send word that they have caught Jack the Ripper. He is residing near a barber's shop upon West Green Road, in southern Tottenham, which is where you shall find the Inspectors now. There is a carriage waiting outside if you are prepared to come right away.'

'Thank you, constable,' replied Holmes. 'We shall come immediately. I am glad we shall travel by carriage, for the likelihood of your superiors getting the better of me in such a deliciously complicated case is a trifle overwhelming.'

Our journey was spent in a rather tense silence. For almost the entire duration, Holmes was consumed by a restless agitation, the slender tips of his long fingers not resting in their customary position just beneath his chin, but consistently patting together upon his lap.

'Holmes, if you are confident that the Inspectors have not bested you, why are you in a state of the most apparent frustration?' I enquired, my patience finally reaching its end.

'Guilt and truth are two entirely separate entities, Watson,' said he, turning to face me with a touch of apprehension in his voice. 'The suspect whom the Inspectors believe to be Jack the Ripper is almost certainly not our man: I base my assumption purely upon the basis that it was *they* who caught him. Darling Jack is perhaps too cunning and devious to be caught by anyone, let alone the bumbling and incompetent prowess of the Lestrade and Abberline. That unfortunately does not mean, my dear fellow, that a case cannot be put forth against the suspect. If Lestrade and Abberline have what they consider sufficient evidence against this man, they will arrest him and they will attempt to prosecute him. They may not even believe entirely in his guilt, but such is the nature of the human condition that glory and vanity will cloud their judgment. They define their success according to a conviction, Watson: I define mine according to the truth. These principles do not only work in tandem but often in parallel.'

'Surely they would not wish to hang an innocent man just to claim an ending to this chapter?' said I, disgusted at such a notion.

'That will be dependent upon the case they can formulate, and their belief in this man's guilt.'

'Here we are, gentlemen,' said the driver as we pulled up outside a small barber's shop. The street was narrow and uninviting, and though there was no apparent cause for such trepidations, it inspired a feeling of ill-will. Wealth was clearly not earned in abundance in such a neighbourhood, but it was clear that money could be earned if you were in a *suitable* trade.

We exited the carriage swiftly, and Smith immediately escorted us down a small passageway, the odour of damp brick pressing down upon us, as if the walls themselves were closing in. We were soon free from this unpleasant corridor, only to find ourselves climbing a treacherous flight of stairs. Mercifully, our journey soon terminated, as we stopped upon threshold of the suspect's quarters. Upon entering, I noticed that the room was small and sparsely furnished: there was a bed, a table and a lamp; covering these essentials were numerous personal items. The walls were bleak, the curtain no more than a ragged old sheet. Sitting upon the bed was a man with piercing blue eyes, and a formidable moustache: his features were nothing short of devilish. Upon the table lay a black top hat, behind the door a long black coat. He wore fashionable trousers, a white shirt and black tie, and patent boots. Filling the room were Inspectors Abberline and Lestrade, as well as Constable Warrington, who stood commandingly over the suspect.

'Well, Lestrade, Abberline, who have we here? Jack the Ripper, I presume. How thrilling it is to finally make your acquaintance,' said Holmes, glancing around the room before cordially extending his hand.

'The pleasure is all mine, Mr. Holmes,' said he, in a deep, grumbling Eastern-European accent.

'Jack the Ripper, a Polish immigrant: that will appeal to the minds of our social Darwinists and adherers to the fallibility of the English class system. *Of course* he was an immigrant, they will proclaim! No Englishman, not even one of our lowliest peasants, could have committed such atrocities! Wouldn't you agree, Abberline?'

'It certainly will appeal, Mr. Holmes, and for good reason!' barked Abberline, sensing that Holmes was not going to be easily convinced.

'Now now, Inspector, you should not be so narrow in your suspicions. If Watson and I can be suspected of being Jack, who is to say that even you are innocent? Now, gentlemen, please present me with the facts.'

'This, Mr. Holmes, is George Chapman,' said Lestrade.

'Would I be correct in my deduction that this man is no relation to Annie Chapman, and also has multiple identities?'

'May I enquire how you know that information?'

'The man is Polish and has coined a new name, Lestrade. His choice of a commonly found family name is presumably so he can simply be lost amongst the numbers. There is no reason for him to be related to Annie Chapman, and his features bear no resemblance to her whatsoever. Please continue.'

'Well, nonetheless, you are right, sir. He is also known as Severin Klosowski, Ludwig Zagowski and Smith. He has posed as an American—'

'A Roman Catholic and a Jew,' finished Holmes.

'That is correct. You *are* familiar with our prisoner, then?'

'By no means, I had simply observed the shape of a kippah protruding from underneath that pile of clothes upon the floor, while the suspect is currently wearing a distinctively Catholic cross around his neck.'

'Ah yes, you are quite right. I thought for a moment you were about to reveal you had your line upon our catch this entire time,' chuckled Lestrade.

'There is still ample time for me to cast your fish back into the sea, Lestrade,' said Holmes. 'I have heard this man's various identities. Please provide a case before we decide what is to become of this most vicious of creatures.'

'Mr. Chapman is a learned man of medicine,' injected Abberline. 'He studied in Poland before coming to England at the conclusion of 1887, and is therefore more than capable, on an anatomical front, of committing the murders which we have seen. Mr. Chapman also has a noted history of violence toward women, as well as what can be described as an insatiable appetite for the pleasures of the female sex.'

'Indeed,' said Holmes, closely scrutinising the man during every word of Abberline's account.

'Our suspect,' Abberline continued, 'had not long been in residence in our capital before we experienced the horrors of 1888. At the time of what I consider to be the first murder, Mr. Chapman was residing in George Yard Whitechapel Road, a mere stone's throw away from where the body of Martha Tabram was found. Regardless of our conflicting views upon that particular matter, Mr. Holmes, you will have undoubtedly deduced that this was nonetheless a perfect location as a base within the Whitechapel area.'

'Have you interviewed Mr. Chapman's wife?' asked Holmes, to the astonishment of all in the room.

'We have,' said Abberline, regaining his composure. 'I left her with one of my men while we awaited your presence.'

'Were you able to extract any useful information from her?'

'Only that she claims Mr. Chapman was with her upon the night of the latest murder. But that is yet to be proved; she could easily be protecting her husband,' answered Lestrade.

'Mr. Chapman,' said Holmes, eyes still transfixed upon the suspect. 'Perhaps you could be so kind as to enlighten us all as to why you failed to mention to the Inspectors here that your current spouse is not the same woman as in 1888?'

'How the devil did you know that?' snarled Chapman.

'I will say nothing other than that you would make quite a terrible cards player. Now, before we continue, is your previous wife still alive?'

'She is.'

'Do you know where she resides?'

'I do.'

'Please divulge such information, Mr. Chapman: it will make our job much easier. I should hate to see the authorities step outside, Watson is really rather disgusted by this whole affair and was informing me just this morning upon new methods of inflicting excruciating pain. Of course, as a doctor, he is also privy to all the nasty little tricks to keep the victim conscious for a sufficient duration of un-pleasantries. I imagine Jack the Ripper would be an ideal test candidate.'

'She lives with her sister and my daughter, Cecilia, at 26 Scarborough Street.'

'Lestrade,' said Holmes, removing a sheet paper from his coat and penning a brief note, 'send a plain-clothed officer round and have him deliver this to the former Mrs. Chapman. But for now, pray continue with your narrative, Inspector Abberline.'

'As I mentioned, Mr. Chapman was ideally situated to carry out the murders. But, what is more intriguing, is that in 1891, the year of your supposed demise, Mr. Holmes, our man relocated to America, and more specifically, to New York. It therefore may not come as a great shock if I were to inform you that soon after landing in New York, a series of rather shocking and disturbing murders took place of an all too familiar nature. Not only this, but it appears that Mr. Chapman has not been long returned to our great nation. He re-emerged in the summer of 1892, a period that curiously coincides with the ending of the New York murders.'

'I wasn't there yet, I was still on the boat,' Chapman gruffly interrupted. 'You can't prove any of that, and you know it.'

'Do you have an explanation for his apparent hibernation between 1892 and now?' said Holmes, ignoring the suspect.

'Not yet. Perhaps he simply wished to allow the waters to quieten down before he rocked the boat once more.'

'It would seem you have a somewhat coherent theory, Inspectors,' said I, in response to what appeared to be a far more convincing suspect than I had anticipated.

'Indeed, I am also impressed,' said Holmes, beginning to pace up and down the cramped room. 'However, may I enquire into the whereabouts of your facts? Your theory is an elegant one, but it will not bear scrutiny unless firmly reinforced. Not even you, Lestrade, can arrest a man based purely upon the shaky grounds of coincidence.'

'Coincidence is a shaky ground now, is it, Mr. Holmes?' said Lestrade, irritated at the smirk now upon Chapman's face. 'It's alright for you to throw such notions in our face but when it is used to convict a man you failed to get to first, we must tread carefully. How rich indeed.'

'I do not have to carry out the formalities of the law, Lestrade. Now, your evidence, gentlemen,' retorted Holmes.

'Oh, don't worry about that, Mr. Holmes,' said Abberline, withdrawing from his pocket a steel box similar in length to a cigarette case, though slightly wider. 'Here is all the evidence we need.'

Holmes took the box and examined it carefully, holding it inches from his nose. Satisfied with his findings, he carefully flicked the small latch upon the side and examined the contents. To an ignorant observer, he may have just examined a featureless piece of wood, such was the lack of expression upon his face. But with what I noticed to be the vaguest hint of an understanding smile, he closed the lid and handed me the box. It was lighter than I expected, and the metal was cool upon my skin. I imitated Holmes's action but could deduce no useful information from the container itself and carefully opened the latch to reveal the contents inside.

I had fully anticipated the kind of evidence which awaited me, but this did not prevent a small feeling of repulsion. Lying inside were four slender fingers and a thumb, delicately cleaned and laid out to resemble a hand. Upon the fourth finger was a small ring, constructed using almost worthless metal, yet manipulated in such a way to suggest it was the work of a once masterful craftsman.

'I assume these fingers match those missing from our victim?' I asked.

'Fingers?' said Chapman, a note of anxiety in his voice for the first time since our arrival. 'What are you talking about? What fingers?'

'You know full well what we are talking about Mr. Chapman,' replied Abberline. 'The missing fingers of our victim, found in the home of a man with a history which is a little too dark and a little too coincidental for my liking!'

'He's put those in here!' Chapman cried, only just being held at bay by Constable Warrington.

'And may I enquire how you discovered your suspect?' said Holmes.

'We had a letter from a rather concerned citizen who lives around these parts,' said Abberline, which seemed sufficient to quell any rebellion left in the suspect. 'He told us that he is well acquainted with Mr. Chapman's wife, and had not seen her for some days. Upon his enquiry as to her condition and whether he would be allowed to visit her, he was met with a very curt response. He alerted one of our men, who came here straightaway, to find Mrs. Chapman being held captive in a most unpleasant manner. You see Mr. Holmes, Mr. Chapman's been poisoning his wife with quite a familiar substance: though I'm sure a clever fellow such as yourself can figure that one out. It was upon arrival and after a bit of background research that we discovered the true nature of our prisoner. I searched the place while Warrington kept guard over our man in here. I found the fingers under a loose floorboard, but thought I would wait for the arrival of the great Sherlock Holmes before unveiling them,' sneered Abberline gleefully.

'I see. In that case I must congratulate you upon the discovery of our first genuine suspect gentlemen,' said Holmes, turning to leave. 'I am indeed most impressed with your work; however, I must urge a word of caution for you not to proceed too hastily.'

'I beg your pardon, Mr. Holmes,' said Abberline, a look of pure fury upon his face. 'This is not merely a suspect. We have conclusive proof that this man, George Chapman, is Jack the Ripper! Did you not hear the facts?'

'I heard the facts, Inspector Abberline, but perhaps I was the only one who was listening. Your man is a prime candidate, that I do not dispute, and perhaps a jury may find him guilty. But pray, answer me this: upon the night of the double murder, Jack the Ripper murdered a woman, was interrupted, fled across London, and then mutilated another. After this, he carried a piece of blood-stained apron, whilst surely covered in blood himself, back across the city, where he left the evidence in an alleyway. He then purposefully risked being sighted in order to scribe a message upon a wall, loosely inciting blame upon the Jews, before disappearing into the night. Not only did the Ripper achieve this, but did so whilst evading capture from the police; avoided reliable detection from a witness, and left purposefully inadequate clues which only suggested falsities, while leaving none which would reveal his true identity. You are now telling me gentlemen, the same man sits before us, finally incriminated, because he could not be bothered to adequately hide or dispose of a few fingers within the confines of his own home?'

'He was bound to get too arrogant after a while!' cried Lestrade.

'Whatever his other flaws, complacency does not appear to be something Jack the Ripper has ever been guilty of. For instance, we still are no closer to identifying our victim; we have a body in Whitechapel with missing fingers: these fingers then just happen to turn up in the home of a rather convenient suspect. You claim they can convict this man, but in reality they tell us nothing and could have easily been planted in this room. Other than the poison, how can you link Mr. Chapman to the most recent murder, when we have no clues as to her identity? Can you prove that he had arrived in America before the New York atrocities? Can you prove his whereabouts upon the night of the previous five murders? Is the alibi given by his wife the truth? You must be certain of the facts before you proceed.'

'Preposterous!' interrupted Abberline. 'We have conclusive evidence that this man is guilty. We may not have investigated all lines of enquiry yet, but I assure you once we have you will eat your words, Mr. Holmes! Then perhaps you will be man enough to admit that Lestrade and I have got the better of you this time.'

'I am simply voicing my concerns, gentlemen,' remarked Holmes coolly. 'I believe for an Inspector to begin the formal procedures of the law before gathering all of the facts is a crime in itself. Proceed as you see fit, but I must warn you that I shall not be privy to your prosecution if you act before you have a complete understanding of the situation. I will not aid in any man being wrongfully sent to the gallows. I shall await your further findings with a keen ear, but for now I must return to Baker Street for an interview with the former Mrs. Chapman.'

# 8

# COUNTING THE CARDS

I OFTEN FIND myself gazing out onto the everyday life which so readily passes by our rooms at 221B. Observing the constant stream of human activity is a pastime of simplicity, and offers an effect upon the mind similar to any meditation. The majority are dictated by profession, their stride urgent and full of purpose; while a fortunate few simply saunter by through course of leisure. Occasionally one of the crowd will stop upon our threshold, shuffle their feet, brush their coat or indulge in some other form of stress-relieving ritual before there is a soft ring of the bell, followed inevitably by a distinctive set of footsteps upon the stair: authoritative, tentative, blustering or casual; all for the express purpose of a consultation with Sherlock Holmes. The variation in step naturally reflects not only the attire but also the manner of the guest.

Having been an intimate friend of Holmes for so many years, one begins to develop a keen sense of deduction regarding a person prior to what most believe to be the necessity of actually laying eyes upon them: speed, volume, pitch; all give distinct clues as to the temperament and wealth of prospective clients. As a rule, unannounced visitors carry themselves in a way which suggests they are desperately clutching to the final tether of their wits. For these poor souls, Holmes is their last fading glimmer of hope: a flicker of light so faint upon the horizon, so tantalisingly real yet distant that such a projection is often self-diagnosed as a mirage; a last cruel trick of the mind before being swept into a swirling damnation of eternal despair. Only upon very rare occasions have I witnessed Holmes cast away such cases, for even if he is not willing to become actively involved, he will, as matter of course, offer advice of such effortless elegance that our guest will leave in a condition of complete disbelief: astonished that the solution to what must have previously seemed an impossibly intricate problem, could ever have been so beautifully simple.

Being in the privileged position I am, I have witnessed Holmes at his best upon countless occasions, but it would be a total fallacy to claim such a picture as the ready norm of our life together. He often bemoans tranquillity as completely insufferable, insisting that his mind needs constant stimulation to prevent it rebelling against stagnation. Though the chemical solution found in his tubes is preferable to those in his needle, he is still testing to live with.

For days now, Holmes had been locked away in his room, a great blaze of smoke pouring constantly from his pipe. I heard him marching endlessly up and down at an often frantic pace. The only intervals I observed in such behaviour were during rather curious periods of low mutterings and theatrical cries; his disposition had taken on such a disturbing turn that one would guess he had either taken to the consumption of a very powerful and dangerous hallucinogenic, or was rehearsing for some twisted and obscene stage production of Dr. Jekyll and Mr. Hyde.

During this time, Holmes received only a single visitor; all others having been abandoned, left desperate and alone. Lucy Chapman had arrived a few hours after our return to Baker Street. She was a slight woman with a subtle beauty that one felt could be enhanced significantly through change of circumstance. Though it was clear her blouse and skirt were her only suitable garments for such a visit, she wore a stern expression, which instantly informed us that she was a proud woman. One gained the impression that she was quite glad to be rid of her former husband, and had no desire to be re-entangled in any of his affairs.

Despite the rather more important issue at hand, I could not help but muse to myself how such a woman became wed to a man like George Chapman.

'Mrs Chapman? I am Sherlock Holmes and this is my friend and colleague, Dr. Watson, please take a seat,' said Holmes though much more impatiently than his usual manner.

'Thank you Mr. Holmes,' she said accepting his invitation. 'Your note said that you wished to discuss an urgent matter of delicacy with me?'

'That is right: it concerns your former husband, who is currently being detained by the police.'

'I do not wish to involve myself in the affairs of that man ever again,' she replied coldly.

'Quite understandable, I only ask you to clarify one or two details. We have heard that he is something of a womanizer, was this the case during your marriage and specifically during 1888?'

'It was.'

'So it was not a rare occurrence for him to be absent from your lodgings during the night?'

'No.'

'Good. Now onto your travels,' Holmes continued, ignoring Mrs Chapman's raised eyebrows at his unusual response. 'Do you recall a set of highly violent murders occurring in New York, similar to that of Jack the Ripper, around the time of your arrival?'

'Jack the Ripper?' she said, a dawn of understanding beginning to seep across her features. 'No, I believe those crimes took place while we were still on our ship. It may interest you to know though Mr. Holmes, that my reason for returning alone from America, was because my former husband threatened me with a large blade, and threatened to sever my head from my shoulders.'

'Do you have anything else to share with us?'

'I believe that is all.'

Such was Holmes's mood he merely rose from his seat, and tossed her a sovereign.

'Watson will show you the door,' said he, not caring so much as to mask his disappointment, before sinking back into the depths of his tobacco-filled cocoon.

'I do apologise for my friend's behaviour,' I said gently, escorting Mrs. Chapman down stairs. 'As you can imagine he is under a great deal of stress, and is often far more courteous to his guests, especially those who aid him in his investigations.'

'It is quite understandable Dr. Watson,' she replied, turning to me with a reassuring smile. 'If you have had the misfortune to meet my former husband, then you are more than aware I have had to deal with a great deal worse than curt dismissal.'

I waited with Mrs. Chapman and watched as the hansom took her away from Baker Street. When I returned upstairs Holmes remained in his room, and I had barely a fleeting glance of him over the next few days. If he was not consumed by his own thoughts in the haze of his quarters, he was in an almost identical state at Pall Mall, lost in a world of schemes, logistics and tedium with Mycroft. Never have I known the two enigmatic siblings to spend such vast quantities of time together, but such was the scale of the problem before them, I was convinced it would require the utmost of both men to conjure a tangible solution to this darkest of puzzles.

I had no interest in suffering the condescension which I was likely to be subjected to when in the presence of two Holmes, and instead decided to be the Baker Street representative at the trial of George Chapman. Holmes, already convinced of the outcome, refused to attend; but I at least wished to witness this most historic of events. I do not believe there is a single man who could have elicited such a public outcry; perhaps only if Napoleon himself had been made to stand trial could such heights of widespread indignation have been achieved.

The galleries were full: the streets packed with thousands of fascinated onlookers, all desperate to lay eyes on the man who could well be Jack the Ripper. I learnt from Lestrade that Chapman was detained in solitary confinement in the Tower before being moved in the dead of night to the Old Bailey, where he was once again placed under lock and key. The legal proceedings were completely formulaic, and little would be gained from scribing such tedious details; however, there are two aspects of interest, which gained much attention at the time, and which I shall include in this chronicle.

The first remarkable feature, so far as the public were concerned, was that Sherlock Holmes would not only be absent from the viewing balcony, but more significantly, he would not be appearing for the prosecution. Holmes's relationship with the force, though occasionally a little jaded, had always been one of courtesy and respect: he had no interest in personal glory, and made it a matter of insistence that his name should not be mentioned in any instance, save for my narratives. The Chapman trial was remarkable, as it marked the only occasion that Sherlock Holmes had to publicly separate himself from the side of the authorities. As to be expected, the reaction was one of confused indignation. How could the man who many considered to be *the* authority on criminal activity, a man who was known to be working alongside Inspectors Lestrade and Abberline, *not* be appearing for the prosecution? Seeds of doubt had been planted into fertile ground before Chapman had even risen from his chair; if Sherlock Holmes did not believe in the man's guilt, how could he *possibly* be guilty?

It was a decisive and fatal blow to the authority and integrity of Inspector Abberline's case: never have I seen lines of such pure animosity dominate a man's face when Holmes announced his decision. The terrible contortion was sufficient in itself to quell any doubts I had harboured about the plausibility of Inspector Abberline being capable of performing the violence of Jack the Ripper. I was overcome by a mixture of pity and incredulity as I observed the manner in which Abberline spat retorts at Holmes in a truly monstrous fashion. My sympathy derived simply out of the anguish the man must have been suffering. To be in a state of almost uncontrollable rage, whilst Holmes's countenance remained in a state of total passivity, must have been unbearable. Though Lestrade, too, was disappointed, he was far better acquainted with Holmes.

My presence at the trial was perhaps an unwelcome reminder of the unpleasantness which had so recently taken place, and I was the attention of several awkward enquiries from the press, which I either refrained from answering or handled in a fashion of the utmost delicacy. It was a most unfortunate situation which had evolved between Abberline and Holmes, particularly within the confines of this most public of environments. It was therefore with great embarrassment on my behalf, and huge frustration for Abberline when the verdict was given. George Chapman was found not guilty for the crimes of Jack the Ripper, due to a lack of conclusive evidence. He was also successful in his claim that he had been innocent of poisoning his wife, and that the man who tried to frame him as the Ripper must also be responsible.

I had attempted to leave the courthouse as swiftly and discreetly as I could, but in a fit of malice, Abberline accused me of sneaking off to the press in order to get the first word and boast before the nation. I am proud to say that I did not take the bait, and simply declined to comment further than that the verdict speaks for itself, before forcing my way through the crowds, back toward the unusual salvation which Baker Street so readily provides.

Upon my return to 221B, I found Holmes in consultation with a thoroughly dishevelled and filthy-looking young street-Arab. His name was Wiggins, the leader of the unofficial foot-soldiers known as the Baker Street Irregulars, a group of miscreants Holmes paid to enact covert operations in our great capital.

'Ah, Watson,' said Holmes, delicately perched upon his customary chair. It was the first occasion over the past several days that I had ample opportunity to scrutinise his notably worn and paler features; his countenance bore all the signs of one bordering upon manic-psychosis. 'You have just arrived to hear young Wiggins' report; it is of really quite some interest.'

'I had almost entirely forgotten your errand, Wiggins,' I said, taking my seat next to Holmes and looking up into the grubby face of our comrade. 'The scent has been cold for so long that I had assumed your task had been a fruitless one.'

'Indeed it 'ad bin sir, tha' is 'til very recent. Sir,' said Wiggins.

'Pray, please describe this most intriguing of gentlemen,' said Holmes.

'Well Mr. 'olmes, our location is a 'ouse of assignation on Regent Street, one of those well-to-do places, where rich folk, married or ovverwise, get up to all kind of promiscuous activities. I 'ave 'eardtha' there is a regula' visitor of this establishment named Mr. Cecil Kirkby. He is a wealthy man, but one whose fortunes are rumoured to be very much on the decline. I hear he is not in a position to continue such meetin's and tha' is why recent 'e terminated these arrangements. Two things are important, Mr. 'olmes; first, the young mistress 'as disappeared, an' second, Mr. Kirkby appears rather unstable. 'e 'as shown unexpected violence and been 'eardmakin' ill-conceived mutterin's. Wha' I 'ear, Mr. 'olmes is tha' Mr. Kirkby's mental 'ealth is goin' very much the same way as 'is finances.'

'When did you learn of this man?' asked Holmes, his eyes closed and his hands drawn.

''e came to our attention abou' a week or so ago. I've bin askin' 'bout 'im and followin' 'im since.'

'Indeed. I wonder, Wiggins, whether you have heard any rumours regarding the possibility of this man having contracted syphilis?'

'None, sir. The decline in 'is 'ealth 'as emerged out of nothin'.'

'Your reward shall be doubled if you can locate this gentleman and have him sitting opposite me before the day is through,' said Holmes, springing from his chair and pacing the room. 'Tell him, I have heard of his predicament and wish all to remain a matter of the utmost privacy. Should he wish his affairs to continue to be so, he should be here as soon as he is free of any other obligations. If he causes you any problems, direct him toward the very public trial which I remained absent from, and the unfortunate attention he may receive if he forces me to consult with him under much more official circumstances; I am sure that, after the spectacular miscalculation of recent events, the authorities will be more than cooperative in supporting me in such matters.'

'Understood Mr. 'olmes,' said Wiggins, as he scurried out of the door back into the busy London streets.

'I assume the verdict was as expected?' asked Holmes, briefly halting his relentless march before the mantle-piece in order to procure some tobacco from his slipper.

'Indeed it was,' said I, keeping a watchful eye upon his habits; I could not offer an explanation for what was nothing more than instinctive intuition, but there was some minor detail in his manner which was somewhat unnerving. 'As we know, there is a long way to travel before an inherently violent man with no alibi in 1888 can be accused of being Jack the Ripper. Regarding more recent events, a neighbour gave evidence that he saw Chapman enter his dwellings at midnight upon the night in question. Chapman had been returning from a local drinking establishment, which was verified, and no contradictory evidence was given to that of his wife, who said he slept beside her in a drunken slumber until morning. In conjunction with the fact that the victim remains anonymous, it is of course impossible to satisfactorily link her to Chapman or anyone else for that matter. Abberline was distraught. He is still convinced of Chapman's guilt regardless of the verdict, and I am afraid to say that all he has achieved is publicly dragging his name through a considerable amount of dirt.'

'That, I am afraid, cannot be helped. If our colleagues insist upon ignoring our kind offers and, as you say, dragging themselves through the dirt, there is little we can do to stop them. Inspector Abberline's was a case of the most deplorable kind: he lacked both evidence and truth. However, not all is lost; now that the authorities have so extravagantly miscalculated, we shall at least enjoy priority over investigations.'

'What are your plans?'

'We have one plan available to us: it is fantastical in both its level of crudeness and personal danger, but now is not the time to discuss such matters. We must be careful, Watson; we cannot afford to commit the kind of ill-judged blunders which our colleagues seem to insist upon. Every step, no matter how trivial or mundane, must be considered to the utmost of our abilities. I shall therefore not even contemplate explaining such a plan until we have heard the curious tale of Mr. Cecil Kirkby.'

~

It is a most un-enjoyable experience to be Holmes's fellow lodger when he is in a period of limbo during a case; his mood resembles that of a man trapped in purgatory. I learnt long ago that any form of diversionary proposal is completely pointless in such circumstances, no matter how practical a recommendation; nothing short of a crisis is sufficient to prevent Holmes from constantly revolving the facts.

During the hours in which we awaited Wiggins' return, he demanded an absolute breakdown of the trial; he was adamant upon hearing every single piece of minutiae. Fortunately, I had prepared for such an event, and had recorded what seemed to be every word of the proceedings. However, in a moment of rare and foolish optimism,I had failed to anticipate that Holmes would not be satisfied to merely read my report, but would insist upon my spoken narrative. It was both tiresome and monotonous, but it helped liberate Holmes's faculties, freeing him to fully visualise my words. Some may find it surprising that he requires such aid, but even the greatest of minds rely upon tricks and techniques to maximise their efficiency and capabilities. Although this kind of request is quite common within the confines of our friendship, I soon became exasperated at Holmes's insistence upon repetition of such vast quantities of ostensibly innocuous data.

By the time we had completed this downright tedious task, I was in a state of utter irritability: a frame of mind which was not helped by the sudden burst of sharp discords that erupted from Holmes's violin. I am grateful that occasionally he accedes to cater for my taste in popular music, and often I am rewarded with performances of quite breathtaking beauty. He commands a delicacy of touch which allows notes to resonate exquisitely in the air before crisply breaking into splendid and supremely controlled staccatos; it was the fluidity and entirely natural transformation in style which informed me I was being left the undeniable calling card of a true musician.

Unfortunately, the balancing act of equal contrast that can be seen throughout our universe was still at work inside 221B, and the price to pay for these sporadic private performances was the torture upon the ear of Holmes' inaudible thrashing of the strings. To suffer this most atrocious of toneless assaults was an all too regular occurrence, and one for which I believe Holmes should be forced to attend Confession. However, such is the affect it has upon his ability to contemplate matters of subtlety, it is regrettably effective.

Under such tumultuous conditions, it was difficult to ascertain as to which one of us was more thrilled by the reappearance of Wiggins and his most intriguing of companions. Mercifully, Holmes placed his violin back in its case and silently swooped back down upon his chair in anticipation, while I exhaustedly gave up my pretence of attempting to read the evening paper.

Mr. Cecil Kirkby could not have wished for a more inappropriate escort upon his first and indeed singular visit to Baker Street. As the two unlikely compatriots entered our rooms, his contrast to Wiggins was starkly apparent. Kirkby struck me as a rather odd fellow: he had an exceedingly strong jaw, which looked as if it would be rather more suitable upon the work of a sculptor. He was clearly not a man of great age, yet the tips of his feathers were prematurely whitened. He had watery green-grey eyes, and wore his fashionable suit with a pompous demeanour.

'Mr. Cecil Kirkby,' said Holmes, rising from his chair and offering his hand to our guest. 'I am Sherlock Holmes and this is my friend and colleague Dr. Watson. Please take a seat.'

'I'll leave you gentlemen to your business,' said Wiggins from the doorway.

'Thank you Wiggins,' said Holmes, discreetly rewarding our Irregular as he shook his hand in farewell before closing the door. 'I apologise for this request of your time on such short notice, Mr. Kirkby, and I offer my sympathies that I have robbed you of your meal: naturally you are not accustomed to such events, but if our interview is brief, you may still make the performance of your treasured Verdi at the Royal Opera House.'

'Have you been having me followed, Mr. Holmes?' demanded our guest, half-rising from his chair.

'That would be a most unnecessary task, Mr. Kirkby, I deduce all from what I see before me,' Holmes replied in a reassuring tone.

'I have heard of your abilities, Mr. Holmes, but it will require more than assurances to convince me of your actions.'

'Very well, a brief demonstration. You are dressed for an evening's entertainment in recently purchased attire from Ede & Ravenscroft: yet it is too early for you to have been journeying to the Opera House, making an early treat of fine cuisine a more likely pre-show destination. A treat which, judging by the uneven shine upon your shoes, will soon become a luxury of the past, as you have recently been forced to let go of your servant and perform the task yourself. How did I know you were going to a performance of Verdi, you may ask? Well, I have heard the offering at the Royal Opera House is quite exceptional, which raises the counter-proposal of where else would a man of taste go on such an evening? If I needed any further assistance upon the matter, I noted the distinctive ticket slightly protruding from your pocket. The enforced curtailing of your expenditure combined with your attendance of Verdi would therefore suggest you are a great admirer, for you can no longer afford the extravagance of choice.'

'Correct upon all accounts,' said Kirkby, though clearly agitated that personal information could be extracted with such apparent ease.

'Now, Mr. Kirkby, I would like to assure you that so long as your activities have remained within the boundaries of the law, and I am not placed in a position where I am obliged to act against you, this interview will remain in the strictest of confidentialities.'

'I appreciate your assurances, Mr. Holmes,' said Kirkby, in a soft, rather curious tone. 'Though I only have a vague inclination as to the reason of your summons, I can guarantee there has been no wrong-doing on my behalf. If I may be so bold, gentlemen, my time is yours, but I would not wish to be inconvenienced for longer than is strictly necessary.'

'Do not worry,' said Holmes, retaking his seat. 'I shall not take up any more of your time unnecessarily. It has come to my attention that you have experienced a case of notable misfortune, specifically in reference to a woman you have been courting. I appreciate the delicacy of the situation,' Holmes answered, in response to the look of irritated surprise upon our guest. 'I simply wish to hear your tale of recent events, and what you believe is the cause of this rather unexpected disappearance.'

'Well, Mr. Holmes, I do not know how you gather your information but you appear remarkably well informed, and I have nothing to hide. I am a bachelor, residing alone in my apartment just off Russell Square. I am a solicitor by profession: I graduated from Cambridge with first-class honours and worked several years as a law clerk. I used the money which I had earned, as well as that acquired from my modest inheritance, to start afresh in establishing my own firm. My work was initially slow, and I struggled to pay the rent on my Lincolns Inn office but through continual success and strokes of good fortune, I made a comfortable living. The majority of my income was through an illustrious client, who shall remain anonymous. I lived a life of comfort and pleasure when I was not absorbed by the anxieties of my work; I have never taken to the temptations of substances or gambling, which are responsible for numerous examples of my colleagues' misfortunes. One matter, which I will confess as it seems pointless to hide my situation before gentlemen already privy to such information, is that I regularly visit a house of assignation upon Regent Street. For concerns of privacy, I travel to this establishment by carriage. I shall not go into details but I should wish merely to state that, though I am not impartial to the notion of marriage, I do not visit such an establishment in the hope of achieving such an end.'

'We are not here to pass judgment upon your way of life, Mr. Kirkby. Cigarette?' asked Holmes, holding out a slender silver container.

'Thank you,' said Kirkby, cheerfully accepting the offer. 'Establishments like this are useful for people of a certain class, where discretion is assured and a certain amount of decorum is still observed. I was a regular visitor for some years before I was acquainted with a Miss Elizabeth Sutherland.'

Our guest paused briefly in order to gather his thoughts and appreciate the calming effect of tobacco; it appeared the events had been most traumatic.

'May you describe this woman for us? I assure you it is of the utmost importance,' said Holmes.

'She was a most attractive woman. She had long blonde hair, a small, rounded face and blue eyes of dazzling beauty. She dressed in a manner which was modestly flattering; never had I seen her wearing so much as a ring which was not perfect in suitability.'

'May I interject with one enquiry before you continue,' said Holmes, his eyes locked upon our guest. 'Why is it that you refer to this Miss Sutherland, whom you so fondly describe, in the past tense?'

'You appeared to be so wise as to the situation, that I admit I had rather assumed you knew what had happened to Elizabeth,' said Kirkby, a flush of anger seeping into his previously relaxed state.

'I was under the impression that Miss Sutherland had disappeared, Mr. Kirkby; unless there is some information which you have failed to share with us, I must ask that you refer to her in the present tense, if only to avoid unnecessary suspicion.'

'Of course,' said Kirkby, through, to my surprise, somewhat gritted teeth. 'While she was married, I had admired Miss Sutherland from afar, but such was the reputation of her husband that I did not wish to trouble myself with either of their acquaintances. After his death, Elizabeth was left with an insufficient inheritance to maintain her previous lifestyle, and to my delight began to visit Regent Street in the hope of finding a suitable courtier. I offered her such means, but I had no real interest in the taking of a wife: particularly in light of more recent developments, which had seen my career embark upon a steep decline.'

'If you are in search of sympathies, Mr. Kirkby, having just informed us of the way in which you would so cruelly manipulate a young woman's heart purely for your own indulgences, I should inform you that you shall receive none. Now continue with your narrative and please stick to the facts.'

'I should inform you, I am not used to being addressed so bluntly, Mr. Holmes! But very well,' he conceded in response to my friend's unimpressed glare, 'I did not fall down a slippery slope professionally, but rather walked off a cliff. I had a single, rather embarrassing mishap while handling a case for the illustrious client I previously mentioned. Since then, I have been struggling: my client abandoned me in an instant and did not hold his tongue regarding my sole instance of misjudgement. I tried to maintain a public appearance and continue my previous social activities to the best of my abilities. I wished to convince Elizabeth to move away with me, out of London, and settle down to a new life of quiet prosperity, but she soon disappeared. I received no warning of her departure and have had no contact; no one seems to have any inkling as to where she may have gone.'

'You say that you attempted to gain this woman's hand in marriage, that she has disappeared, and there are no decipherable clues as to her location, and yet only now, under my invitation, do you divulge such information. Why have you not come to me sooner?'

'I only courted her hand as I did not want to begin a new life in complete solitude.'

'You are fortunate your actions are not punishable by law, Mr. Kirkby. You are a despicably selfish man who deserves nothing less than the severest of Her Majesty's punishments.'

'And who are you to judge me, Mr. Holmes? You are hardly renowned for your love of women!'

'There is a difference between mistrust and manipulation to an appalling degree,' said Holmes coldly. 'But come, let us not play games; there is less mystery surrounding Miss Sutherland's fate than you appreciate. It seems apparent that she has chosen a man of much higher calibre, and from your descriptions, I am sure such a woman would not find it difficult to attract a desirable suitor; after all, if she had heard of your professional predicament and read between the lines of your fickle attempts at winning her hand, why would she choose to settle for such apparent mediocrity?'

'Mediocrity!' bellowed Kirkby leaping to his feet, hands clenched in fury. 'I have never been slandered by such language in my life! If she has chosen another man, she has done herself a great disservice!'

'Ahh, we have touched upon a nerve, have we not?'

said Holmes, remaining calmly in his seat. 'You claim to have no particular feeling for this woman, yet at the slightest hint that you are unworthy of her companionship, you become quite deranged. A curiously violent disposition, is it not, Watson?'

'Most curious, Holmes,' said I.

'You will not speak to me this way!' cried our guest.

'Oh, I do not believe it is your ego that we are worried about upsetting, Mr. Kirkby. No matter what façade you may use to try to fool us with, it is quite apparent that although you enjoyed toying with this young woman's emotions, you were actually deeply in love with her. In your own shameful way, you may have even believed you were being charmingly aloof. A great shame to have lost her, I am sure, but fret not, I am sure she is being looked after by a far worthier candidate.'

I cannot recall another occasion where there has been such a scene inside our quarters. Most men whom Holmes backs into their respective corners accept their plight, and submit into a state of passive inevitability; Mr. Kirkby, however, displayed no signs of rationale, and we were given a violent demonstration of just how unhinged he had become. Upon Holmes's final taunt, Kirkby flipped the delicately arranged tea table laid by Mrs Hudson, sending the china cups and crockery crashing down upon the floor. Holmes and I were on our feet in an instant, but such was the condition of our man that it was more like engaging a wild and untamed beast. Blows were cast with such uninhibited violence that it was clear our man had become quite deranged; Holmes and I both suffered considerable knocks before we had restrained our man once more.

'I think we should simply tie him for now,' said Holmes, wrapped around Kirkby on the floor in some form of foreign stranglehold. We tied our man's ankles, thighs and wrists, and left him writhing upon the floor like some pathetic serpent as we regained our composure. 'Now that we have indeed experienced your violence, Mr. Kirkby, I would like you to entertain yet another theory of mine, for I must confess that I have been rather dishonest with you. What would you say if I were to tell you that I know exactly where your beloved Elizabeth is?'

'Fiend! Tell me where she is this instant!'

'I believe you already know her whereabouts, do you not, Jack.'

'Jack? What is this? Who are you talking to?'

'I believe I am talking to Jack the Ripper, am I not?'

'Jack the Ripper? Are you insane?'

'Ah, come now, Mr. Kirkby, you must surely know that Miss Elizabeth Sutherland is lying, perfectly preserved, upon a stone slab in Whitechapel Mortuary. After all, are you not the man who poisoned her, and then defiled her body with nothing but a long sharp blade?'

'You lie!' screamed Kirkby, before breaking down into sobs of unmitigated horror.

'The victim is Elizabeth Sutherland. I would take you to see her, but I am afraid it would be a most unpleasant experience. You remember her eyes, don't you? Those blue eyes of dazzling beauty: it really is a shame Jack the Ripper gouged them from their sockets. Who knows what he will have done with them: after all, he previously claimed to have fried and eaten a victim's kidney.'

'Enough,' Kirkby wept in a barely audible manner. 'I am not Jack the Ripper.'

'That is yet to be seen,' said Holmes, pacing around the slithering wreck upon our floor.

'I was forced to reveal my secret! I don't know how he found out but he did! He told me to make sure that you heard about my case through your little gang. I was to convince you I was losing my mind. He told me if I did not comply then he would *kill Elizabeth!* … and myself,' he added, as an almost insignificant afterthought.

'Who is this man?' said Holmes, kneeling over Kirkby's head and piercing him with his gaze.

'I did not see him. I had been at Regent Street until a late hour; he picked me up from outside, disguised as a cabbie. He locked me inside and took me to a deserted yard. He held me at gun-point but it was an unusual weapon, with some form of strange extension upon the barrel.'

'It was most likely a silencing device,' said I, 'used for muffling the sound of a shot.'

'Well, only the barrel and this silencing device protruded through the barrier, I could not see his face. He gave me my instructions and forced me from the cab, abandoning me in the yard. He told me if I tried to pursue him, he would not hesitate to shoot me. I had no desire to follow.'

'Why did you not tell me this when you first entered the room instead of carrying out this foolish charade?'

'He told me he would know if I did not comply! I did not dare risk such a chance. I was to convince you I was mad, he gave me three options Mr. Holmes.'

'Insanity, suicide or murder,' finished Holmes.

'You know the man of whom I speak?'

'Did he give you a name?' asked Holmes.

'Yes… Professor James Moriarty.'

~

There is little more to tell from our interview with Mr. Cecil Kirkby. The man was entirely incomprehensible, such was his recent trauma. It took some time to convince him that the latest victim of Jack the Ripper was not Miss Elizabeth Sutherland. Although he would still have to accept the far more likely truth that his love had departed with another man, it was at least of some reassurance for him to know she had not been mutilated by the most infamous of criminals.

What was of far greater significance was his final revelation: one so profound and shocking in its nature that Holmes had simply stood there silent, before retiring to his room, leaving me to deal with the broken man upon our floor. When Holmes finally re-emerged, his countenance was grave, and he was quite visibly disturbed.

'You do not honestly believe Moriarty survived Reichenbach?' I asked as he glided silently across to the windows and drew the shutters.

'If there was one man other than myself who could have survived such a fall, it was Moriarty.'

'But I thought you had a plan of action? Will you allow all those hours spent with Mycroft simply to go to waste because a man whom we had not even heard of until this afternoon, claimed to have been threatened into a task by Moriarty? It could quite easily have been Moran.'

'You are right, Watson, there is only one way to be sure, –through decisive action.'

'Will you share this information with me?'

'Tonight I shall be in command of my very own specially trained force. All most secret, of course: Abberline and Lestrade are not trusted with such information but they will be informed.'

'You expect to weasel out Jack the Ripper with a team of specials?'

'Hardly, Watson; the weaselling, as you so eloquently put it, will be entrusted to a far more suitable and far less official force.'

'The Baker Street Irregulars?'

'Who better to flush out a criminal than a gang of criminals? Mycroft and I have devised a plan of action which allows for the complete exploitation of both these agencies, and of course, we shall also have our part to play, the most dangerous of parts.'

'Holmes, this is fantastic news!' I cried. 'What is the plan?'

'Patience, Watson, patience. First, I believe it will be an entirely worthwhile exercise if we were to recount all of the facts as we have them, to ensure that the plan is indeed viable. If you could fetch a pen and paper while I rearrange the furniture, then I shall cast my thoughts out into the air for you to catch upon your parchment.

'Now, the first five victims were all women of the night, and all were successfully identified. None of the bodies showed any evidence of a struggle or robbery. The violence of each crime, excluding the first of the double murder, always increased with the next victim. Only upon the occasion of the double murder was there any attempt to place blame, which I believe to have been a purposeful act of arrogance and diversion. Previously I believed these crimes not to have been random but meticulously planned and executed by Professor Moriarty. Is there anything I have missed?'

'I believe that is all the facts,' I replied.

'Good. Now this recent victim is an anomaly. She was not a lady of the night; she has most likely been dressed to appear so, and her identity remains unknown. The victim was poisoned and taken to the scene of the crime: she was therefore not a victim of chance but of choice, though we are still nonetheless wiser as to why this was the case. The effort taken to remove identifiable features from her person is also suggestive, and presumably there is something regarding her identity which will aid us in unmasking Jack the Ripper. Previously I would have been inclined to follow the assumption that the man Kirkby described was, in fact, Colonel Moran. But now I am not so sure, for we are still missing an agent capable of committing the recent crimes. Kirkby was a pawn: he did not have the stomach for such horrors. I am certain that he was not threatened into performing the monstrous deeds under the alias of Jack the Ripper.'

'You believe there is a missing agent?'

'It is the only logical conclusion of the facts. We have two hypotheses, Watson: Moran used an agent that has escaped our attention or Moriarty has indeed returned.'

'Though more plausible, the latter is still surely far-fetched?'

'I never saw Moriarty's body, Watson, therefore we have no concrete evidence that he did in fact perish.'

'Do you have a theory as to a motive for all this?'

'Fear, Watson, pure and utter terror on an unimaginable scale.'

'Whatever do you mean?'

'The one scenario that we failed to recognise: we provided Moran with an alibi upon the night of the latest murder. It is a fairly safe assumption that he did not anticipate his capture or that he was in fact destroying a wax-bust of myself. If we therefore assume Moran's involvement in the logistics of both my assassination and the return of Jack the Ripper, I believe we have our motive.'

'Good God! The murder of Sherlock Holmes and the return of Jack the Ripper upon the same night. It is unthinkable!'

'I see no other hypothesis to fit the facts: Moran knew of, or at least suspected my survival. If Moriarty is indeed still among us, he may have passed on this terrible design to lure me out of retirement and slay me in cold blood while he himself resurrected Jack the Ripper in all his infamy! Moriarty would have his revenge, and strike a fear so deep into the hearts of our citizens that they would barely brave to step outside their own doorsteps. A rather neat little plan, I must admit.'

'I fail to see how any plan of action can cater to the facts you have just laid out; all you have done is made it more than clear how little progress we have made.'

'Sometimes, Watson, if you wish to catch an illusive fish, the best course of action is to set fire to the sea.'

'You are going to set fire to London? What a brilliant plan! Are we going to shoot any survivors? Poison the water supply? I just hope Jack the Ripper has not simply gone on holiday, we may destroy the city for nothing.'

'I do not mean literally,' said Holmes, slightly amused. 'We will force the Ripper out by beating him at his own game.'

'Beat him at his own game: Holmes, what on earth have you been planning?'

'Later tonight, the streets of Whitechapel will be littered with the bodies of mutilated and disembowelled women. Jack the Ripper always acts in the same area, and he will be forced to quench his murderous thirst, for if he can do so and avoid capture in such an environment, it would surely be his greatest triumph: or quite simply, he shall fail.'

'Holmes, that is absurd! You cannot tell me that you are willing to mutilate women just to capture this man!'

'Do not be blind, Watson; we use the Baker Street Irregulars and a very select group of volunteers. Wiggins and his gang shout fire all over Whitechapel, the 'bodies' will be put in place and quickly sealed off. Maximum attention is drawn to the scenes, panic ensues yet no one is any the wiser. This will happen simultaneously all across the district. Contact has been made with all late-night establishments: they have agreed to keep their custom inside, other than a select few, all of whom are armed and being shadowed by a special. This practice is already in place: the disguised specials swap station every night to avoid detection, as do the women, which is of course entirely natural under such dangerous conditions. He will not be prepared for such an event, and will be forced back into finding a victim of convenience, of which we shall know the location of every possible candidate, and we shall unmask him; Moriarty or otherwise. If he is not lured out, then I have made arrangements with Lord Balmoral to print the rather lurid descriptions which I have conjured for him; the public will believe that the Ripper has been recruiting, but his ability to shock them will forever be substantially diminished. It is desirable that this should not be the case but it could well be a risky, yet worthwhile deception.'

'Holmes, what if Jack the Ripper simply goes to another part of London and enacts his revenge there?'

'That would be a most unfortunate occurrence, I admit, but I do not believe he would do so. Remember the audacity of his actions upon the night of the double murder; remember how he specifically brought a victim to Whitechapel before he murdered her. Unless I am very much mistaken, his pride will not allow this challenge to go unanswered.'

'When do we ignite this bomb of yours?'

'Tonight. We shall journey to Mycroft's, and from the comfort of his quarters, we shall set the capital ablaze.'

# 9

# DINNER AND A SHOW

THE UNMASKING OF Jack the Ripper was a subject that the entire civilised world had been fascinated with for many years. The brutality of his actions was caught up in a grotesque and perverted admiration, not only for the audacity of his crimes, but also the ease with which he evaded both capture and identification.

My excitement at the prospect of ending this most disturbing of chapters was combined with an almost fearful reluctance. It is one thing to chase a demon through the valleys of damnation, but to finally pull back the veil and stare into the soulless sockets of this hellish spectre would require all the courage I could muster.

Sherlock Holmes did not cater to such theatrical notions; but I remained unsure how even he, the foremost man of logic and reason, would respond once truly in the presence of this most demonic of criminals. I could not help but shudder at the thought of a resurrected Moriarty and the consequences this would have upon my great friend; but still, even if confronted with this greatest of fears, I suspected Holmes would refuse to balk in the face of the devil and would instead rather simply shake his hand.

We remained silent throughout our journey to Pall Mall, but I was certain it was thoughts along these lines which dominated Holmes's mind: if he could conclusively place Professor James Moriarty and Jack the Ripper into the chronicles of history, it would be a professional feat of truly monumental proportions. He would certainly refuse any credit or public admiration, but his contributions would surely be placed amongst the greatest this country has seen. Perhaps one day, Holmes would be seen looking out, ever vigilant, across the city, immortalised by his own column.

We arrived outside Mycroft's lodgings at nine o'clock. As we exited our carriage, we were blasted by the cool crisp bite of the night air, an irritating drizzle as its companion. Holmes remained convinced that the Ripper would continue to act only after midnight,for if he were to alter from such a pattern, it would diminish the audacity of both his crime and escape. Accordingly, he argued, our time would be more constructively used discussing the finer details of our approaching task, and I suspected that the formalities of dinner, insisted upon by Mycroft, were only agreed to purely for my benefit.

We were welcomed at the door by Geoffrey, and shown into a room dominated by a splendid oak table: there were only three seats present, and it was apparent that two of these had only recently been put out. Holmes had previously informed me that Mycroft's distaste for visitors was such that he only acceded to hosting political meetings in the most important of circumstances. If further evidence was required of such a notion, the room was rather blandly decorated with just two portraits: one of Lord Palmerston, the other of Pitt the Elder. We were soon joined by our reluctant host, and though Holmes predictably ate very little, Mycroft and I enjoyed a splendour of culinary triumphs. We were treated to a light helping of spinach soup, soles au gratin and pigeon stewed with mushroom. This was followed by the wonderful offerings of both lamb and salmon, served with potatoes, asparagus, salad and whole beans. To finish our meal, we had strawberries and cream, accompanied by some truly fine Cognac. I must admit that our surroundings were entirely inappropriate for the course our evening was about to take, but if we were to be roaming the streets of hell in search of Jack the Ripper, I was acutely aware this supper could well be my last.

Such was the occasion that Mycroft, to my delight, offered Holmes and I one of his H. Upmann cigars: a truly fine smoke, which he had saved from the previous year. We made our way into the sitting-room to discuss matters in privacy, away from any possible interruptions or potential eavesdropping by the servants, and each took a seat by the fire.

A large map of Whitechapel was placed on the table between us, three vultures surveying the scene before swooping down upon their prey. Carefully marked were the designated positions of each would-be victim; unlike previous instances, it would be necessary for our decoys to be in places of relative exposure, so as to create as great a panic as possible. The outer net and bait for the trap encompassed four locations: the first destination was south of Whitechapel Road in a Goods Depot yard between Lambeth Street and Gower's Walk. Our eastern location would be close to London Hospital and Medical College, on the Turner Street end of Green Street. The northern site would be at a brewery on Carter Street, just off Brick Lane, and completing the encirclement to the west was a Van and Cart Works, situated between Fournier Street and Fashion Street.

I admit that upon first hearing this aspect of the plan, I thought it was leaving far too much to chance, for I had momentarily forgotten that we also controlled the exact location of the only women permitted to go about their business in the Whitechapel area. These women, who were being paid handsomely for their endeavours, were only allowed to operate within the secondary ring; all other night-walkers had been subsidised for their private incarceration. Such was the desperation of these women that they had previously been forced to risk the Ripper, in order to earn enough income simply to survive, and it was imperative that he should not find such an opportunity this night.

The trap would begin at the Osborne Street end of Whitechapel High Street: it would run east until running briefly north up Bakers Row, where it would turn west down Hanbury Street before dipping south down King Edward Street, opposite the church of the latest murder. Here the trail would once again turn west down Chicksand Street, which would finally turn south upon Brick Lane and merge back into Osborne Street and thus completing the trap. It was within the confines of this secondary inner-ring where Jack the Ripper would be forced to find his prey; policemen would patrol the area in their usual formulaic routine in no greater numbers, so as not to arouse unnecessary suspicion.

'So what do you think of our design, Watson?' asked Holmes, a look of triumph upon his face.

'It is indeed a comprehensive plan; I believe the subtlety in which you avoid simply flooding the area with men yet control virtually every movement within, could well prove a masterstroke,' said I, retaking my seat and enjoying the fine sensation my cigar had upon dampening my nervous stimulation. 'Where shall we be placed?'

'We shall be disguised, patrolling the streets; we will travel separately into Whitechapel and remain detached. I feel we would be rather wasted in a lookout post, and our purpose shall be better served if we are dispersed.'

'Excellent,' said I. 'What about the two Inspectors? I assume that they will have roles to play.'

'Lestrade and Abberline will both be situated at the church: it offers a certain strategic advantage and they shall be able to see out into the streets from high above, while no one will be any the wiser for their presence. It is important that neither of them, particularly Abberline, is seen wandering the streets, or it shall give the game away. I am also anxious to ensure that he would not be left to his own devices, Watson, as I knew that it would make you uncomfortable.'

'I am pleased you take my suspicions so seriously. I know it is far-fetched, but as a former soldier, I am more than aware just how crucial one's instincts can be. I assume on account of your usual habits that you shall remain here, Mycroft?'

'Indeed you are correct,' said he, doing little to hide the tone of monotony in his voice. 'Someone has to remain upon the sidelines; every theatre of war needs a director.'

'Of course. Holmes, do we have any idea where he is likely to strike?'

'There is a school which runs alongside Old Montague Street and St Mary Street. Unless I am sorely mistaken, I believe that, given the opportunity, and having only recently acted so deplorably outside a church, the Ripper would quite fancy the defilement of a school. We must patrol and hope that we can lure him into the comforting darkness; it is there that we shall at last come face to face with Jack the Ripper. But that can wait until this evening,' said Holmes, swiftly making toward the exit. 'before I descend into Whitechapel, I have a few points of interest which I wish to discuss with Lord Balmoral, should our plan prove unsuccessful. Watson, your hansom should arrive shortly after mine and return you to Baker Street. Another will then arrive at precisely eleven o'clock to take you to the East End.'

'I never was able to comprehend why he spends so much time running around,' said Mycroft, after Holmes had disappeared into the night's now heavy rain. 'I believe once you have reached a certain intellect, it is far easier to let others exert themselves in such a fashion.'

'We cannot all remain idle, Mycroft,' I said, buttoning my coat. 'Even you have already been busy planning with Holmes.'

'Ah well, he only came to me from time to time. I was a consultant, not an orchestrator, and such a distinction is immaterial: the current plan of action could not have been improved. I hope to see you both triumphantly return here later this evening, so that I may inform the Prime Minister that we are finally at the end of this ghastly affair.'

I rattled along the streets of London toward the East End disguised in a dirty, bushy beard, a long shabby coat and a flat-cap; a fully-loaded revolver as my only companion. I had found further instructions waiting at 221B: I was to take the cab as far as Whitechapel High Street, where I would complete the journey on foot into the inner-ring of the trap. I had no designated area to patrol, only to remain aware that I should not linger.

Though my night had the potential to become exceedingly dangerous, I could not help but allow Holmes' behaviour to consume my thoughts. Mycroft's last remark had rather struck me, for I could deduce no reason why Holmes would deceive me: his usual custom in such a circumstance is to divulge to me no information at all.

I stepped out of the hansom and began my steady march into Whitechapel; the cold, relentless downpour caused the matted hair of my beard to press irritably against my face. I made my way down the road, but such were the conditions that I almost walked straight past Great Garden Street. Confident that it was virtually impossible to have been followed in the almost impenetrable darkness, I continued on into the very heart of the trap, ever vigilant for any signs of Jack the Ripper. Quite how Holmes expected to even sight, let alone catch the Ripper in such circumstances was not apparent, for half my attention was upon my every step. I decided to briefly take shelter in a nearby alleyway, no longer certain as to my bearings. Such was my appearance that it was not difficult to adopt the role of a homeless man, so I slumped back upon the threshold of a closed butchers' and waited.

I am not sure how long I remained stationary: my muscles began to shake and my bones rattled in response to the fierce chill blowing in the night air; the old wound in my shoulder began to throb as a reminder that my suffering can always intensify. Painful though it was, I was convinced that it was less suspicious to have taken shelter than to be still seen wandering the streets.

I remained alone in the dark, content to allow the rain to pour down around me. My mind began to wander as I continued to squint into the all-encompassing dark canvas. I could not help but contemplate the chaos which was likely to ensue if our night's adventure was to fail. Such is Holmes' brilliance that this is thankfully a rare consideration, but never before had we encountered a criminal mind so singular.

I stood up in an effort to prevent the inevitable stiffness from rusting my joints, and pulled my coat tight around my neck, when I suddenly noticed the silhouette of a figure in the distance. It was impossible to ascertain any notable features of this lurking shadow, so I left my post.

Instantly I was struck by the bitter howl of wind, and almost lost sight of my man. I quickened my pace, a terrible instinct driving me forward. My haste almost cost me dearly, for when I arrived into the square, I was forced to instantly drop to the ground. Peering out into the darkness, I could now clearly see his outline: he wore a long black coat and top hat. I was certain that he could not see where I lay, but fear had taken my body. I was possessed with a great urge to flee; but no sooner had I dismissed such a treacherous notion than the Ripper turned and disappeared down a narrow passageway.

Determined that Holmes would not have to combat this monster alone, I leapt to my feet and continued my pursuit, running down the minor incline of an adjacent alleyway. The Ripper had quickened his pace and was almost out of sight as I rounded the corner. Unnerved by this sudden development, I momentarily glanced down the passageway from which he had descended. All that could be seen in the darkness was what appeared to be a solitary arm, lying lifelessly in the alley. My heart filled with trepidation. I approached the body, and to my horror, noticed a stream of blood flowing down the street. There was a man lying in the gutter: his innocent eyes staring blankly into the night sky, a terrible laceration across his throat. Constable Smith was the first victim of the night.

I could not help but stand and look upon Smith's tragic face; he had gone to the races but been thrown to the wolves. It was clear that he was beyond aid, so I turned and ran down the street where I had last seen the Ripper, fully conscious that there was now an unguarded woman roaming the streets of Whitechapel.

Unsure where to even begin my search, I frantically scoured my immediate surroundings for any indication of where to turn, when Holmes's earlier prediction dawned upon me. Continuing my pursuit down a side-street, I ran on through the darkness before coming to an abrupt halt; there in the distance was Jack the Ripper, dragging the lifeless body of a woman into the school. Desperate to atone for my failure, I was determined to bring an end to this most heinous of chapters. I withdrew the revolver from my pocket and made haste toward the entrance. I was just about to enter, when I was suddenly grabbed and swung round by none other than Sherlock Holmes.

'Holmes, what the hell are you doing?' I cried, outraged that he had allowed the Ripper to walk straight past him.

'Quiet, Watson! Or you shall give the game away,' he urgently whispered. 'We must proceed with caution; we have him in our sights.'

'But what about the woman?'

'The woman is most likely dead, Watson; we cannot help her. Now follow my lead.'

Silently, we crept into the school, the door not so much as creaking under Holmes' delicate touch. Finally we were out of the open, and plummeted into a muted silence; only the elements could now be heard, banging upon the windows. We went through an open doorway into an abandoned corridor; the cheerful patter of playful feet had long since vacated this haunting building. Empty classrooms, filled with single desks were no longer occupied by innocence and mischief, only hollow spirits. There was a dull glow at the end of the hallway, and we soon came to a small room.

Standing with his back to us was the devilish figure of Jack the Ripper. He stood, arms by his sides, an eight-inch blade firmly grasped in his right hand, dripping with the undeniable crimson of fresh blood. On his right, laid upon a small table, were his other demonic instruments of savage mutilation. Holmes took out his revolver and gradually edged his wayforward. The Ripper descended murderously over his victim, when suddenly, Holmes grasped him by the throat, revolver to his temple.

'I think that is quite enough, don't you,' said Holmes, forcing the Ripper to his knees, *'dear brother.'*

Such was my shock at this statement that I confess I almost fell to *my* knees.

'Mycroft?' I exclaimed, forcing myself past in order to confirm Holmes's accusation.

The sight which awaited me was one which would cause the icy grip of fear to clasp even the stoutest of hearts. Previously in the evening, Mycroft's eyes had been their usual watery grey: cold, calculating, yet human. Now I found myself staring into the malevolent chasms that were the eyes of Jack the Ripper. I almost balked when confronted by this sight. Screams, visions of torture and terrible violence pierced my vision, as though the victims themselves were trying to escape from their hell.

'*Bravo* Sherlock,' said Mycroft, a subdued and subtle violence penetrating his usually lofty tone. 'I thought I had hoodwinked you yet again.'

'Holmes, what is the meaning of this?' I demanded, raising my weapon and aiming it at point-blank range into the temple of the Ripper.

'Calm yourself, Watson! We shall move ourselves into a room of more comfort and leave this unfortunate woman.'

Never have I seen looks of such pure menace. Sherlock and Mycroft Holmes locked eyes with hatred so fierce that I became unnerved at the prospect at meeting either gaze; it was clear they were now brothers only by blood.

'The girl is alive, Holmes, and merely unconscious,' I said, relieved.

'The girl is not important, Watson, leave her. She is safe now and we have far more pressing issues to attend,' said Holmes, his barrel never so much as an inch from his brother's skull as he led Mycroft out and into another of the abandoned classrooms.

While I blocked the only exit, Holmes forced Mycroft onto a chair, before lighting two lamps and taking a seat behind a large desk, his revolver rested upon the surface, aimed directly at the heart of his brother. As I joined my friend and took a seat at his desk, I could not help but admire his ability to completely detach himself from his cases: never would I have believed it possible for even he to remain in a state of such total composure.

'Come, Sherlock,' said Mycroft, visibly amused. 'How long have you known my little secret?'

'Since our visit to George Chapman,' said he, lighting a cigarette.

'Holmes!'

'My goodness, it took you that long? Come, dear brother, perhaps you were lost at Reichenbach after all.'

'Holmes, you have known the identity of Jack the Ripper for over a week, and you have not confided in me? I am appalled at your lack of trust!'

'Do not be hysterical, Watson,' said he. 'You are fully aware that you have my complete trust in these matters; however, this was a problem of such delicacy that I needed to be absolutely certain of my conclusions. Would you have ever been able to look at me in the same light again if I had wrongfully suspected my own brother of such crimes? The trust and foundations of our friendship could be shattered, and I would have been no closer to my goal.'

'Yes, yes, of course... I am sorry.'

'You deduced your conclusions from the fingers, I presume,' said Mycroft, an air of boredom his only response to my outburst.

'Of course.'

'Holmes,' said I. 'How could you have possibly made the link from those fingers to *Mycroft* being Jack the Ripper? They contained no remarkable features.'

'That is not so Watson; the fingers were certainly remarkable, and it was precisely because I *knew* they had been planted that I told the Inspectors that they *could* have been. I did not wish to share my suspicions, but I hinted at least at the more than likely weakness in their theory; but alas, they did not listen.'

'But how on earth could you have been certain?'

'Because, Watson,' said Sherlock Holmes, his gaze briefly meeting my own. 'The fingers found in the lodgings of George Chapman once belonged to Irene Adler.'

'Irene Adler!' I cried, as haunting visions began to torment my mind. Flashes of dainty elegance, delicate beauty and kindly grace were fiendishly twisting into visions of horror: the slashed throat, the eyes, the torn face and ripped body. A woman of such magnificence, ungraciously slumped, murdered in a church doorway. How could any man commit such atrocities? Even for someone of Mycroft's detachment, surely this was a step too far. To defile any woman in such a manner is the act of a sadistic coward, but to have ripped apart such beauty and robbed the world of such a singular woman without so much as a glimmer of remorse was more than I could withstand. 'Holmes, even for you, surely that is a farcical conclusion: how could you have deduced this information with such insufficient evidence?'

'The ring, Watson, it was the ring. It was made of a distinctively valueless compound, but the craftsmanship made it rather unique. Miss Adler had acquired it as a token of appreciation from a once-great tradesman who had fallen upon ruin; there is no doubt that it was her.'

'Ah yes, I thought you might have needed a bit of a *helping hand*,' said Mycroft, allowing himself a singular, perverse laugh.

'I would advise you keep such comments to a minimum, Mycroft,' said Holmes, as I cocked my pistol. 'I may not be willing to allow Watson to sacrifice himself in order to see you brought to justice, but do not for *one second* believe that I shall not personally accompany you into the depths of hell, if you so push me.'

'But this is impossible, Holmes!' said I.

'Have I touched a nerve, Sherlock?' mocked Mycroft. 'I thought you were above such common flaws. It must have been quite difficult for you to discover the truth. I hear she was quite the woman, *the* woman, one might say. Unfortunate that someone so remarkable shared the same end as those other wretched hags. You should know that I was quite gentle with her, Sherlock. I thought you would appreciate a more delicate touch.'

It is impossible for me to accurately describe the expression which had intruded onto my friend's face: never have I seen such malice. It was as if all human emotion had drained from his being, leaving his countenance to bear the resemblance of one completely void. Yet despite this vacancy, there was something in the depths of his aura, a calculated and murderous fury which simmered ferociously behind his eyes. He made no move, and simply sat still, transfixed upon his treacherous brother. I had always harboured a minor suspicion of Holmes's true capabilities, but I had been able to laugh off certain inklings through the comforting knowledge of our friendship: never again could I dismiss such trepidations.

'I wish it were impossible, Watson,' said Sherlock Holmes, toneless in his response. 'But as I have told you before, once you eliminate all possibilities, that which remains must be the truth. I have spent my time since my enlightenment contemplating counter-theories, but none would suffice. I do not believe in ghost stories or the supernatural; the idea that this mysterious man could have been Moriarty was a hypothesis I could not accept. It had to be someone else, an agent with the intellectual prowess and power to achieve such a feat, and Mycroft was the only man alive capable of toying simultaneously with both Moriarty and myself.'

'That may be so, Holmes, but why would Mycroft wish to commit these atrocities?'

'A lowly priest has to look after his flock, does he not, Dr. Watson?' said Mycroft.

'What the devil do you mean?' I demanded, as Holmes appeared quite content to lazily sit back in his chair and smoke whilst his brother divulged this most shocking of tales.

'Journey back to 1888, gentlemen, and the great game being played by my dear brother here and the late Professor Moriarty: the great detective, the *foremost man of the law,* was being beaten, Dr. Watson!' said Mycroft, with a most sickening smirk. 'Professor Moriarty was arguably the most dangerous criminal mind the world has ever seen: he was a threat to this great city and to this country. The stranglehold he commanded had become quite insufferable. As Sherlock has undoubtedly informed you, Dr. Watson, I am the secret-keeper, the central exchange of the British Government. Everywhere I turned, I saw the mark of this man penetrating the very core of this great nation:the cornerstones of our society, age-old institutions were being perversely molested by a man most people had never even heard of! I could not allow this to continue. This man quite simply *had* to be stopped, and if there was one man who could bring this Napoleon of crime to justice it was, of course, Sherlock Holmes! Or so I once naively believed. You failed, Sherlock. That is, until you were given a little extra motivation.

'I hatched an elaborate plan, designed specifically to arouse the full potential of my darling little brother. The crimes had to be *perfect*: meticulous, yet random; savage, yet unmotivated. The criminal must be the most infamous, yet he must never have a face. Jack the Ripper is an illusion, a haunting; he is the embodiment of fear in its purest of terms. He could have been *anyone*! You have seen the reports in the press: he has a different appearance, a different background, a different nationality every week! If I could persuade my *fabulous* brother that this man, the most infamous criminal of all, was also the most dangerous; in Professor Moriarty, I knew it would only be a matter of time before Sherlock Holmes would single-handedly destroy the greatest criminal empire that we have ever seen. No one else could perform this task, Dr. Watson; the authorities would barely entertain the notion that Moriarty was even a criminal, let alone the single biggest threat this empire has ever faced! He was an invisible disease: one which could not be felt or detected until the seeds of decay had grown and devoured their host, leaving nothing but a ravaged, empty carcass. Only Sherlock and I were aware of this most dangerous of threats. What was I to do at such an impasse? We could not defeat Moriarty, for he left no evidence. We needed the chain, Dr. Watson, a decisive link between crime and creator! So I created a diversion. I set out upon weekends as my schedule was often busy. Whitechapel offered the most suitable destination, as it was practically swimming with the kind of deprivation I was after. I auditioned my victims from afar and awaited the perfect opportunity before casting my leading lady. I struck from behind, covered their mouths and slit their throats. I ensured each victim followed a certain pattern, but always allowed for greater violence upon my next outing. It was all rather too easy to throw the authorities off the right scent: they even refused to believe the involvement of an educated man, despite all the evidence to the contrary. How fabulously predictable our force is!

'There were two men in London whose attention I knew I had gained: Sherlock Holmes and Professor James Moriarty. It may surprise you to learn, Sherlock, that the Professor was quite disturbed by the appearance of this demon in his city. Moriarty believed he had the perfect criminal empire and that he controlled all those within it. I heard it drove him quite mad to hear of this Jack the Ripper, for he knew better than most that this was no ordinary criminal. Moriarty had sparked the slow burning inferno, and was quite content to observe as the flames danced around and caressed our society before engulfing it in a blaze of decadence and despair. He did not expect that anything could arise from such ashes, let alone a criminal mind sufficiently devious to challenge him for supremacy of the underworld. Jack the Ripper was perhaps more of an obsession for Moriarty than he was for you, Sherlock. Do not preach false idols; we both know you welcomed the Ripper with open arms. It was Jack the Ripper who provided the crucial distraction and allowed you to grasp your first tangible link. Without him, you would never have defeated Professor Moriarty. So you see, Dr. Watson, judge me if you will, curse me, or perhaps from the look in your eye, shoot me; but ask yourself this, what does it matter if a few prostitutes were mutilated if it meant the long-term security of this country? I did what I did based upon pure reason.'

'Reason?' I spat. 'You are nothing more than a madman with a blade! You may believe that you acted according to logic, Mycroft, but I assure you, you have allowed your mind to become unhinged; you are nothing more than a savage. The greatest men do not cater to thoughts of sedition and murder; you have reduced yourself to nothing more than a disgrace.'

'You are a weak-minded fool if you underestimate the significance of Professor Moriarty's demise. You call me a madman, but all of the women, with one exception, already lived in the depths of despair. You have seen Whitechapel, have you not? You have seen the degradation of this rancid tumour. One day our glorious nation will be rid of such disgraceful places. But tell me, why do you value the lives of the animals which dwell in the pits of hell alongside those which have made our country great?'

'You cannot tell me that defeating Moriarty could *only* be achieved by mutilating women! Had you joined with your brother, your combined intellectual prowess would have been more than sufficient to bring about the demise of Moriarty!'

'The plan had to be far more subtle than that, dear doctor! Moriarty would have seen everything that we threw at him, not to mention the extra time it would have taken. Sherlock and I are always over indulgent when it came to deliberating together; it is far easier to allow him to take the lead and act accordingly. But why should I share the honours with my brother when I could prove that I am the foremost intellect? Listening to the ways in which the entire nation seems to think that light cascades out of his very being, watching Moriarty inconvenience me and cause havoc in my city on an almost daily basis?

Oh no, dear doctor, it was I who would have the last laugh, and would have done had my brother not survived the perils of Reichenbach. As you have witnessed, I had to barely leave my chair to cause the confusion and borderline anarchy of Jack the Ripper; people are even beginning to speculate over ludicrous plots involving the Royal Family. It really is most entertaining.'

'This is madness,' said I. 'You have known Professor Moriarty to be dead for some three years. Why bring the Ripper back and choose a victim that Holmes was almost certain to eventually identify?'

'The Ripper was resurrected, Watson,' said Holmes, 'because, Mycroft had become impatient at my approach toward the Bagatelle-Quartet. He quite simply did not trust in my ability to resolve the issue readily enough. He did not understand the subtleties of my allowing the Park Lane Mystery to drag on, and rather believed I had lost my touch. He kidnapped Miss Adler to ensure that he had the perfect tonic, should I require any extra motivation. He manipulated the entire situation by embroiling Moran and the Bagatelle-Quartet with Moriarty's false Ripper legacy. The use of Irene Adler was to entwine my fate within the state-emergencies which he so desperately needed solving. It is most unfortunate, Watson, that I did not listen to your advice upon that fateful night.'

'Holmes?'

'I rejected your suggestion of alerting Mycroft as to our movements. Had I done so, Irene Adler would still be alive, and Jack the Ripper would have lived forever as a faceless phantom. Though at least now we know the truth.'

'Oh I *wish* that were so, Sherlock, but I am afraid Miss Adler would have suffered her fate regardless of any news; though had you kept me up-to-date, she would admittedly have suffered a rather less conspicuous death. I knew the companion of whom you spoke in your letters from Montpellier, and assumed that no matter what noble warnings you offered, that such a woman would not remain idle. I awaited your return and had some of my men follow you, all upon the lookout for any unwanted attention. They soon discovered a suspicious character who charted your every movement, and they raised my attention. Of course they believed that it was all for your protection, and would never have dreamt that the person they pursued was actually a woman. I did not care for the possible distraction this criminal offered, having read Dr. Watson's account of how she previously bested you. Such a woman was a danger, and had to be removed. Rather conveniently, it transpired that I would soon need another woman for my next exertion, and I saw no reason why I should bother to go out of my way to find and kill another pathetic creature when I had such a fitting candidate standing before me, particularly as she offered the possibility for such an amusing conundrum. Once I abducted Miss Adler, her fate was sealed. I kept her in a secret part of my quarters and used the antimony to maintain her in a sufficiently weakened state. I continued my business as usual, and was prevented the necessity of divulging my secret to anyone else.'

I must confess that I found myself greatly disturbed at the logical reasoning placed before me by Mycroft Holmes: though he was quite clearly the possessor of truly first-class intellect, it was just as apparent that he also possessed a disposition bordering on homicidal-insanity, and he needed to be silenced. I slowly rose from my seat, the barrel of my revolver never aimed so much as a fraction from the centre of his temple.

'Watson!' cried Sherlock Holmes. 'Do not be foolish! I have already lost a brother tonight; do not allow me to lose my one true companion by succumbing to the temptation of emptying your barrel.'

But to Holmes's surprise, I turned and strode decisively toward the exit.

'If you are journeying toward the authorities, I really must protest,' said Mycroft.

'You are in no position to protest against anything, Mycroft!' I shouted, turning back into the room.

'I rather think you are wrong there, Watson,' said Sherlock Holmes, knocking the wind from my sails.

'Holmes,' I said, having finally regained my composure. 'I know that he is your brother but for God's sake, he is also *Jack the Ripper!* We have no choice but to hand him over to Lestrade and Abberline. He cannot go free.'

'I would rather disagree with you there, my dear doctor,' said Mycroft. 'Do you honestly believe that I would have planted those fingers in George Chapman's dwelling if I did not wish Sherlock to discover my secret? Come, I had always believed you were a far more astute fellow than this.'

'You may dress yourself in as much verbal nonsense as you wish, Mycroft, but I refuse to stand here and allow you to walk away! There is not a single reason you can provide which will change my mind.'

'How about anarchy, Watson?' said Sherlock Holmes.

'Anarchy?' I repeated, but even as I spoke, a compromising dawn of light began to break through the clouds of confusion.

'If we go to the authorities and present Mycroft as Jack the Ripper, then the entire country shall descend into chaos. Mycroft Holmes, a man considered by many to *be* the British Government, who has advised the Royal

Family, and who effectively holds more power than the Prime Minister himself, is Jack the Ripper. The uproar would be catastrophic: citizens would never trust the government again, foreign nations would cease to deal with us, the Empire would fall into disrepute, and the country would descend into an impenetrable darkness. So you see, Watson, there is a very good reason indeed not only why Mycroft cannot be revealed, but also why he has chosen to reveal himself only to ourselves, to demonstrate just how successfully he has won, beaten us all, in this most deplorable of games.'

It was not until I had heard the dejected self-admission of Holmes's defeat that I regained my composure and returned to his side. Mycroft had manoeuvred himself into a position of complete infallibility. Jack the Ripper could never be caught. What should have been Holmes's greatest achievement would have to be recorded as his biggest failure. He had mocked others, rejected their theories, and acted in a manner suggestive that he would, as he seemingly always did, discover the truth in a flash of subtle brilliance. Now he would have to live with the knowledge that, in the eye of the public, not only had he failed, but in a manner so unworthy of his great mind that it would surely torment him for the rest of his life.

As I pondered the implications of this turn of events, their significance began to dawn upon me: if Mycroft could not be exposed under any circumstances, he needed to be silenced. I could not allow a man with this perverse form of immunity from prosecution continue his life, with nothing but his own conscience preventing him from terrorising London's streets once more. Though Holmes had previously stated that he would not allow for my sacrifice, I came to the conclusion that there was no viable alternative. If Mycroft was to be stopped, I had to be the one to rid the world of Jack the Ripper. Holmes's life was far more valuable than my own.

As I sat back down, it took all of my concentration to prevent any expression which may have betrayed my true purpose. I gripped my revolver, pondering the consequences of the action I was about to perform. The biographer and intimate friend of Sherlock Holmes murders a top-level British politician in cold blood, for reasons unknown. I confess this was a level of heroïsm I had never expected to burden. I would be tried and found guilty before the entire world and hanged in disgrace. Only Holmes and I would be privy to the knowledge of my noble, yet publicly dishonourable death. The only comforting thought was that I would soon be reunited with Mary. I felt certain the Almighty would forgive my sins and allow me passage into His great kingdom, having slain this most foul and wretched of creatures.

I began to inhale deeply, allowing the oxygen to feed my cells and calm my nerves. I knew I had only one shot, one opportunity to bury my bullet into the temple of Jack the Ripper. I had been covering Mycroft's movements so there would be no sudden rush on my behalf. I steadied my hand and softly began to squeeze the trigger…

'I should of course tell you, Mycroft,' said Sherlock Holmes, suddenly rising from his chair, as if he had sensed my sacrificial intent, 'that though you may have positioned yourself quite brilliantly in relation to the law, you have been rather less successful in beating me.'

'Oh really?' said Mycroft, an air of impatience in his voice. 'And tell me, dear brother, what trick are you about to pull out of the hat this time? I can see no way in which you could have bested me, I have been ahead of you every step of the way for years!'

'Perhaps; but I think you will find that I have enjoyed

the advantage in our more recent contest. First of all, you sent the letter to Lord Balmoral that sparked this whole affair, to bring me back to London in order to investigate and topple the Bagatelle-Quartet. You also arranged for the second letter to be delivered to your lodgings; the man who came to the door upon my return from exile was someone in your service whom you paid to deliver the letter. He was not aware of the contents, or why it was insisted upon that he wore a rather specific and unusual choice of attire. Geoffrey, of course, only reported what he saw, and has no further role to play in this affair. By entwining the fate of the Ripper into that of the Bagatelle-Quartet, you ensured that I would not get distracted and ignore Moran. That much is clear. Now onto more intriguing matters: upon the night of Irene Adler's murder, I sent out lines of enquiry using both official and non-official means. I must admit, it struck me as quite peculiar that Wiggins was completely unsuccessful, for I believed he had the greatest chance of success. It was a problem which continued to baffle me: the woman was clearly of a certain stature; therefore a more notable woman *had* to be missing. I then found it curious that Lestrade and Abberline were rather miraculously drawn to a man with, what seemed to me, an all-too convenient set of credentials. It seems clear that you encouraged a citizen to take on the role of the Samaritan, and that you have had your eyes on a selection of fitting candidates for many years. Of course, after the discovery of Miss Adler's fingers, your purpose was clear: you were single-handedly toying with the entire nation and me. I did not wish to believe that it was you, Mycroft. I can hardly claim our relationship bears any resemblance to one which is close, but the idea that you might be Jack the Ripper was still rather distasteful. But I knew how to ascertain your identity. While we were in the depths of our planning together, I let slip my disappointment in Wiggins's failure to bring me not even one suitable suspect. Only a week or so passed after I divulged this information to you, and then Wiggins placed in my hands the most curious case of Mr. Cecil Kirkby. His mentioning of Moriarty was clearly designed to throw me off the true scent, while, I am sure, giving you much cause for amusement at the thought of haunting my thoughts with the ghosts of resurrected Professors. Your vanity and your arrogance were your downfall, dear brother: you had a slight nibble upon the bait but failed to recognise the line upon the end, and I was now certain as to the identity of the fish I was hunting. The question was then, with my newfound advantage, how best to beat you at your own game. The answer was simple. I needed to acquire a confession.'

'Oh bravo!' cried Mycroft, in mock amusement and boredom. 'I must admit you outmanoeuvred me with Wiggins, but come, you cannot possibly expect to gain a confession out of me. I am afraid it is *your* arrogance that has failed you, Sherlock.'

'I wonder, Mycroft, whether you are familiar with Thomas Edison's phonograph?' said Holmes. He began to fiddle with an inner-compartment of the desk, before extracting a large box-like contraption and placing it on the desk, a visible hint of amusement on his features. 'It is really a rather remarkable invention, used for recording sound. You may also be familiar with speaking-tubes? They are used for communication between the bridge and engine room in steamships, and I have adapted them for my purpose. The phonograph was hidden inside this table, connected, rather ingeniously, to a series of speaking-tubes.'

Holmes turned on the phonograph, and sure enough

we could hear, quite clearly, an earlier conversation: though slightly muffled and a little distorted, the identity of the two voices was undeniable. I had kept my aim firmly upon Mycroft for the duration of Holmes's revelation, but it was only during this development that I ever felt I was performing any worthwhile task; the look upon Mycroft's face was that of pure malice.

'So you see, my dear Mycroft, that although we may have reached a stalemate, should you choose to act unwisely in the future, you shall undoubtedly find yourself in checkmate. I am forced to allow you to continue your life as you did before. You may contact me professionally only if our country is upon the eve of Armageddon. Though I dare say it is unnecessary, I feel compelled to warn you that if I hear so much as a whisper regarding Jack the Ripper, the true Jack the Ripper, I shall not hesitate to expose you. I have been responsible for the destruction of Moriarty and his great criminal empire; do not think that I shall hesitate in bringing you and this greatest of empires crashing to its knees, and watching it crumble and burn into the archives of history.'

# 10

# BAKER STREET

IT WAS A treacherous morning. The rain pounded upon the pavement with such continuous velocity that it appeared the elements were vying to be reunited in an attempt to break through their artificial constraints. A terrible, glooming grey had submerged the city into a sombre mourning; it was difficult to believe upon days like this that we should ever again be blessed with the soothing grace of the sun.

It had been two days since Holmes and I had vacated Whitechapel, and he had been asleep ever since. Quite how he managed this feat, to sleep so soundly and for such duration, only hours after unveiling his own brother as one of the most infamous criminal minds, is a notion beyond my own comprehension. What is more, the public backlash was rather overwhelming. In their eyes, not only had we failed, but Constable Smith had needlessly lost his life. It was a tremendous burden to carry the light of illumination and comfort, yet be forced to leave so many desperate souls standing shivering, tormented in the darkness. We could not even attempt to console Smith's family with the truth. Yet for Holmes, none of this appeared to be of consequence. It would seem that, as long as a revelation is satisfactorily revealed, and a case can be argued not only from start to finish but also from finish to start, he was content to rest.

I could still not quite comprehend all that had passed. I had never been particularly fond of Mycroft, but never would I have dreamt of him committing a crime, let alone the atrocities to which I heard him confess. I was deeply troubled in my conscience. How could I live with myself if he ever chose to indulge his demonic appetite once again? Some may agree with his callous remarks, that women living in the hell of Whitechapel are better off dead; but I am not so inclined. I will not have the innocent blood of any person upon my hands, no matter how deprived their life may be. I cannot say that I was overly surprised to note that it was upon this most woeful of days that marked Sherlock Holmes' emergence from his room. It was as if his very existence thrived in the uncertainty of others, for after all, a life without crime is no life for a consulting detective.

'Have you been asleep this entire time, Holmes?' I enquired as he emerged from his quarters wrapped in his old dressing-gown, and scrutinising a single sheet of paper.

'Certainly not, dear fellow, I enjoyed twenty hours of sleep after our return, and have since been immersed in a most unusual case. See these hieroglyphics,' said he, passing me a sheet of paper, upon which was a series of strange child-like drawings of bizarre little men, dancing across the page. 'Mrs. Hudson delivered them while you were still asleep. They were sent to me by a Mr. Hilton Cubitt, of Riding Thorpe Manor in Norfolk. The drawings were accompanied by a letter, and I am expecting our guest within the hour.'

'Holmes, if I may momentarily distract your attention before the arrival of Mr. Cubitt.' I was unsure how to approach this subject, for I had scarcely thought that it would arise so promptly, but I knew Holmes would not divert his attention once immersed into another case. 'Why was it that after you explicitly said before Mycroft that the Ripper would most likely strike in the school, did he then act exactly as you had predicted?'

'It was all part of the game, dear fellow: Mycroft was of course unaware that I knew his true identity, and so wished to beat me once again, by successfully striking in the exact location which I had predicted. If he were to be unsuccessful however, and therefore suspected I had discovered his secret, he knew I would confront him alone. In either scenario, it was a somewhat low risk for him to take.'

'But how was it that you were able to work the phonograph in that school?'

'Electricity, Watson,' said he, with a look which told me he was only to be asked matters of interest.

'But the recordings of Mycroft, the confession with which the security of your case depends upon, are you sure they are safe?'

'Safe?' said he, seated next to the fire, enjoying what looked to be his first meal in well over a week. 'How on earth can they ever be safe?'

'You cannot tell me that you are going to trust Mycroft's moral compass as the only guarantee to prevent the return of Jack the Ripper?'

'Of course not. You saw the look upon his face; he knows that his little escapades into the streets of Whitechapel are at an end. I assure you that even had he the desire to try and steal the recording, he would find it quite impossible.'

'What do you mean?'

'I destroyed the evidence,' said he, casually sipping his tea.

'You destroyed it? Holmes, what could have possessed you to do such a thing?'

'Come with me, dear fellow,' said he, rising and ushering me into his quarters. He pointed me in the direction of one of his great shelves; placed between two other rather curious objects was the strange contraption I had last seen in Whitechapel. The exit station for the sound looked like an expanded and deformed hollow flower.

'Here, listen to this; scrutinise it closely, and all shall be revealed.'

I did as Holmes asked, and placed my ear as close as was comfortable to the device and listened intently to the recording, keen not to miss any point of subtlety which was so often key to Holmes's little demonstrations. It was of a conversation he had recorded between himself and Mycroft regarding the logistics of their operation. At first, everything sounded completely natural, but toward the end it began to sound rather strange. Mycroft's tone was slightly inconsistent, his pitch not quite perfect.

'Dear God, Holmes that is you! That is what you were doing when I heard your theatrical performances! I must admit I am rather relieved; I thought you were going mad!'

'Ha! Oh no, I knew that if I could convince Mycroft I had such a recording, it would prevent him from acting unwisely; not of course that he would need to, now that Moriarty, Moran and their empire have been successfully buried. Should he attempt to steal the evidence, we may rest assured that he will never find it. It is quite the neat little problem, to destroy that which does not exist. But, regardless, the success of my little performance has no relevance upon the case. Mycroft has had his fun with me these last few years; I merely thought it prudent that I should at least be allowed, as they say, the last laugh. One day, perhaps such methods will indeed exist and aid the more unimaginative and lazy investigators to trap their prey, but for now, we must rely on more unconventional methods of ingenuity.'

'Will we ever be able to chronicle this account, Holmes? Even your innovation toward recorded evidence is of sufficient importance for the public to benefit from, and surely they have a right to know that Sherlock Holmes did indeed save them from the tyranny of Jack the Ripper?'

'No, Watson, they cannot be informed. Even if such a method were possible at this point in time, such an invention in the hands of the wrong person could be used to devastating effect. We have already proven its hypothetical role in advancing the role of blackmail, and I have no intention of speeding up this process. Unfortunately for our dear citizens, they must endure the terror that somewhere, lurking in the shadows, is an unstoppable demon: a spectre which can never be seen and never be caught. One day, you and I shall sit down together in our retirement and scribe this most disturbing of tales but alas, I do not believe that the public will be ready for the shock until long after our deaths. The empire may well have fallen, itself a matter only for the historian, before the world is ready for the horror of my singular confession.'

'But what about the Bagatelle-Quartet?' I urged, 'What in God's name was the plot that drove Mycroft to resort back to such extremes?'

'Oh, that is of little importance! Blackmail, politics, secret-intelligence, it is all very mundane and shall be dealt with in a most discreet manner. But, unless I am mistaken, I can hear a heavy yet purposeful foot upon the stair. Come Watson, I believe we have work to do, if we are to discover the cause behind these rather absurd dancing men.'